Timewalker Chronicles Book 2: Silver Storm

MICHELE CALLAHAN

Timewalker Chronicles, Book 2:

SILVER STORM

by Michele Callahan

© 2014 by Michele Callahan
All Rights Reserved

*Donna—
Wow! Meeting you in Milwaukee was way cool. :)
Michele Callahan*

Ω 3 Ω

Timewalker Chronicles Book 2: Silver Storm

MICHELE CALLAHAN

Ω
SILVER STORM

Lost...On a hot summer night twenty-five years ago a freak lightning bolt struck Sarah St. Pierre on Lake Michigan. Presumed dead, her body was never found. She simply...vanished.

Hunted...Timothy Daniel Tucker retired, but the group of people he once worked for aren't willing to give him up so easily. They watch him, waiting for him to crack, waiting for an excuse to bring him back in to finish what he started.

When Tim finds a beautiful naked woman floating in Hendrick's Lake, he suspects a trap. She claims to be the same woman who disappeared over two decades ago, but she hasn't aged a day. Worse, she knows intimate details about his covert work on a weapon that could destroy all of humanity. Trust is impossible, but Tim will not stop until he discovers all of her secrets, until he uncovers the truth.

Hunted by an unseen enemy, Sarah claims to see things no one else can see, to know things about the future that no one could possibly know. And she has a frightening power no human should wield. Falling in love is an unacceptable risk but Tim can't walk away from her visions, her power, or the fierce desire she ignites within him. Predator or prey? Truth or lies? Love or duty? Decisions must be made. Millions of lives hang in the balance...

...and the clock is ticking.

Timewalker Chronicles Book 2: Silver Storm

MICHELE CALLAHAN

Dedication

For Tom, who never stopped believing.

Timewalker Chronicles Book 2: Silver Storm

MICHELE CALLAHAN

Ω
Chapter One

Friday, 5:17 AM
Glowing silver embers fell from the sky over Chicago and all of her suburbs. The glittering snowflakes spread over the city faster than dawn could shoot its rays of new morning light. Night hung on by her fingernails, the sun trapped behind the horizon for a precious few minutes. The early risers, those who initially believed themselves blessed to witness a miracle, gasped in awe and cried at the unearthly beauty floating down over them like a billion falling stars.

Then the screaming began as everything and everyone, nine million people, burned to ash in a matter of minutes.

Three Days Earlier, 5:17 AM
Silence hovered over the water and a few moments of peace settled over Tim like a cool mist on a hot July day. He grinned and finished tying the spinner on his line. The soft lapping sounds against the side of his aluminum boat, smell of wet vegetation, and honking geese gliding around the edges of Hendrick Lake were as far from the deserted lab, blazing heat and gunfire as he could get. Tuesday morning meant most people were back at work, leaving the lake and the best fishing spots empty…just the way he liked it.

Bandit curled up in her bed on the floor of the nine-foot boat, content to sleep for a few more hours. The tiny Pekingese mix was used to Tim's routine. Fish. Run. Scan the news headlines every night for things he dreaded to see. He'd sit at the computer and she'd curl up in his lap. She did everything with him now. When he'd flown home to bury his parents, she'd been a four-month old puppy he could fit inside his combat boot. He'd come home on six months mandatory leave to *'get his head back in the game.'* The top brass didn't like the fact that his research was turning up nothing but rotten eggs. Nothing was said, but it didn't take a rocket scientist to know they hoped the death of his parents would push him deeper into the game. He had nothing left now but a dog, an empty house and scars. Lots of scars.

Bandit hopped up and yipped at him, happily wagging her tail as if to remind him that he had *her*. And how dare he think he needed anything else? The princess of a puppy had been his mother's whim and a completely spoiled lap dog. The tiny pooch had lived a life of luxury traveling in his mother's purse everywhere she went. He'd considered giving the pup away after the funeral, but couldn't bring himself to do it. That was four months ago. The little girl wasn't much bigger now, a whopping ten pounds soaking wet, but she kept him company, she was smart, she liked to fish, and she was the only family he had left.

"Okay, fur ball. Let's see what we can catch today." Tim cast his line out over his favorite fishing spot and let the spinner sink a few inches before slowly reeling it back in. The rhythm and monotony chased away the last of his lingering nightmares.

Bandit growled low in her throat and paced over her pillow, rumbling like a tiny electric toy stuck in the 'On' position. The hair on her body started to rise, forming a round fluffy brown and white snowball with huge brown eyes. Bandit looked like a cartoon character. Tim would've laughed, but the hair on his arms crackled with static electricity as well and rose to attention like a thousand miniature soldiers. The water puckered as if it were being hit by raindrops, but there were no clouds. No rain. No thunderstorms on the horizon waiting to zap him and his boat into oblivion with a stray bolt of lightning.

Tim reeled in his line and stashed the fishing pole in its spot along the side of his seat. Bandit stood at rigid attention on her fluffy brown bed and continued to growl, a steady little rumble of warning that set his teeth on edge. They were too exposed on the water, too out in the open. He clenched his jaw to keep a stream of expletives from rolling off his tongue.

Perhaps this was a freak storm. There had to be a perfectly good explanation, because if it were the boys from the lab, he'd be dead already. No, whatever this was, it wasn't normal. His silence came as automatic as breathing. He didn't start the small trolling motor. He took out a wooden oar and paddled smoothly for the tree line behind his house. Two minutes, perhaps three, and he'd be under cover. He hoped that wouldn't be two minutes too long.

"Shit."

The electrical buzz building in the air continued to grow stronger until he could hear the slight hum around him. His skin prickled and the water on the side of the boat rose, forming hundreds of fluid stalagmites rising, bursting, and sinking back into the water faster than he could track them.

Earthquake? E.M.P? Geomagnetics? Had those bastards

finally done it?

The electric charge shocked him with static build-up every time he moved. Time to get off the water before whatever was happening cooked him in place or worse.

He glided into the reeds only a few feet from shore and tried to figure out how he could get off the boat without touching the supercharged water. Any second now he expected stunned or dead fish to start popping to the surface. Maybe the Fish and Game boys were doing this for a count or culling of the lake. He couldn't imagine why they would, but they should've posted warnings.

Bandit yelped and sunk to her belly, whimpering and shivering. A thunderous boom filled the air and a burst of silver light to his right blinded him. Instinct drove him to the bottom of his boat for cover. He grabbed Bandit and held her squirming torso down as his mind raced with possibilities.

A bomb? Lightning?

Whatever it was ruined a perfectly good fishing trip.

As suddenly as it all began, it was over. The supercharged air dissipated like it had never been and the hair on his arms returned to its usual resting place. His clothes stopped crackling. The water, roiling moments ago, returned to a serene and placid lapping against the side of his small boat. The geese took up their honking as if nothing out of the ordinary had just happened. Bandit suddenly leaped to her feet and jumped onto the bench seat he'd just vacated. Her curled tail wagged fiercely as she yapped at something just out of his sight.

Ears still ringing from the blast of lightning, he pulled his ever-present knife from its sheath at his waist and lifted his head just enough to see over the edge of the boat.

She floated face up at the water's edge. Unconscious. Naked. Her head was toward shore in no more than three or four inches of water, leaving the rest of her long, willowy body drifting alongside his boat. Was she dead? That's all he needed. Dead body, 9-1-1 call, and fifteen hours at the police station saying, "I don't know," until his tongue was bleeding.

Hell. He didn't dare get in the water and risk immediate electrocution. Bandit had no such inhibitions.

"No!"

Too late. The little wet rat swam happily to the woman's side and sniffed her hair, sopping wet tail wagging like a curled mop waving him into the water.

"You little turkey." With a sigh, he threw the small anchor and then jumped over the side after his crazy dog. He landed in knee-deep water and leaned over the woman, feeling for a pulse. His shoulders relaxed when the steady beat of her heart thrummed beneath his fingertips. Her chest rose and fell, her small, perfect breasts capturing his gaze as they followed the peaceful rhythm of a deep, dreamless sleep. No blood. No lacerations. No bumps on the head or obvious injury. She was, in a word, perfect.

Sun-bleached brown hair floated around her pale face in a halo of dark silk. Full, deep pink lips and dark lashes outlined her features like an artist's brush strokes. A light dusting of freckles gave her a pixie-like quality he found shockingly appealing. She looked like a sun-drenched California beach beauty, complete with tan lines from a itsy-bitsy bikini and a siren's hair. Long hair. Long everything. He guessed she was at least six feet tall, with incredibly long legs, a slender waist, and small tight breasts that would fit his hand to perfection. She was lean, like a gazelle, muscular and slim. Obviously either an athlete or someone obsessed with the gym.

What the hell was she doing naked, floating in a lake where she'd appeared from nowhere like a bad magic trick?

Her eyelids fluttered open to reveal dazed hazel green irises that seemed unable to focus on his face. Her whispered words shocked him.

"Timothy Daniel Tucker."

Three words. His name. His whole name. No one had called him that since his mother had thrown it around the house when he would behave like only a particularly aggravating teenage boy could. He was damn good at aggravating a woman when he wanted to be. At least when they were conscious…

"Who are you?" Tim demanded an answer, but she was out again. So, who the hell was she and why did she know his name?

Regardless, he couldn't leave her in the water. The lake was cold, even this time of year, and she'd get hypothermia. Training kicked in and he lifted her from the water to carry her inside. His house backed to the lake. Five steps and they'd be at his fence, in his back yard. He'd get her inside and warmed up. Once she came to, he'd get some answers. If he didn't like those answers, a phone call and an ambulance ride would get her out of his hair.

Bandit jumped around in the water and swam to shore right behind him, tail still wagging like she'd lost her little mind.

"You know something I don't, girl?" Tim walked under the raised porch and yanked the sliding glass door to his basement open with his thumb. Careful not to bang the unconscious woman's head on the doorframe, he turned sideways and stepped into the rec room in his basement. Suede leather couches. A couple of fat recliners. Giant flat screen T.V., X-Box, pool table, a kitchenette and bedroom off to the side. It was the ultimate bachelor pad. At least that's why he told himself he never went upstairs anymore. Might as well live in a four thousand square foot, five-bedroom museum. Perhaps he did.

Bandit yapped happily and he'd swear the dog was smiling as she trotted after him into the house dripping lake water. Gently as he could, he laid the mystery woman down on his soft brown couch and pulled a fuzzy green blanket from where it rested over the arm of the couch to cover her. He tucked her in like a mummy, a sigh of relief escaping. With her delectable body covered, maybe he could start using his brain again, start thinking about something other than the softness of her skin. He grabbed a towel out of the bathroom closet to put under her hair. The silken mess reached just past her shoulders and was soaking everything in sight.

As gently as he could, he tugged the wet mass out from beneath her shoulders. With his right hand he reached along her neck to cup her head and lift it, sliding the towel beneath her and doing his best to fight with long strands that seemed determined to stick to her skin. Heat pulsed beneath his palm, surged through the soft flesh of her neck, unnaturally hot, but he ignored it for the moment, intent on his goal…getting the wet masses of her hair contained in the towel. Moving the sopping strands on her head around was worse than battling tangled rope. He grimaced at his lack of finesse, absolutely certain he was only making it worse.

"Sorry." She couldn't hear him, but it made him feel a bit better about the hack job he was doing to her head. Towel in

Timewalker Chronicles Book 2: Silver Storm

place, he stepped back and debated what to do next. She'd said his name. He'd never met her before, he was sure of it. The whole thing screamed trouble, and that was one thing he couldn't afford if he wanted to stay off the Sec-Nav's radar. He didn't care who she was, it wasn't worth the risk.

He reached for the cordless phone on the end table and studied her face while he went over the facts again. She wasn't bleeding or obviously injured. No black eye or bruised ribs from a fight with a boyfriend. No wedding band. No marks on her perfect body whatsoever. How she ended up next to his boat in the middle of an electrical storm, he had no idea. But her arrival wasn't normal. There was no *logical* explanation for where she came from or how the hell she'd managed to get that close to his boat without alerting either him or Bandit.

So, that left *illogical* explanations.

He shook his head. No way. He'd destroyed everything. It wasn't possible.

Neither was the feeling he had that he'd seen her somewhere before, or that he'd kill to protect her.

The two feelings were equally unwelcome. First, she was gorgeous. He was sure he'd remember her if he'd met her before. And he hadn't. His life the last ten years hadn't left much room for a woman, and he hadn't felt right asking one to put up with what he did. He'd seen the wives of soldiers wailing in grief too many times to go there.

And protect her? Kill for her? He didn't do that anymore. He'd put in his time. M.I.T.. Army. Then sucked into the world of Intel and weapons development. Eight years fighting bad guys in the field and two more practically locked in the lab. No thanks. That game was over. He'd made sure of it.

9-1-1. Three numbers, a few questions, and she was someone else's problem.

He dialed the numbers, stared at the green 'send' button, then her face. Bandit's head tilted in a sweet mixture of curiosity and all-out adoration as she stared at the woman. "Dumb dog."

He couldn't do it.

"Damn it!" He needed some kind of explanation from the mystery woman. She'd arrived practically on his doorstep, less than fifty yards from his home, in the middle of the most bizarre electrical event he'd ever seen. Curiosity might kill him, but he had to have some answers. If nothing else, if she had knowledge of a new type of electrical weapon or experiment, he ought to report it to the boys at Aberdeen.

Hell, maybe they'd sent her. Maybe he hadn't been as thorough with his diversion and misdirection as he'd thought. He put the phone down and rubbed his hands on his thighs, unsure of what to do next. Gently shake her? Maybe a cold, wet cloth on her forehead? He snorted. Hell, how about a cold bucket of ice water over her head? That'd do the job.

If his mother were here, he'd let her fuss over the mystery woman. But she wasn't here. The thought made his chest ache, so he buried it and sat on the edge of the couch staring. He wasn't an eight year old, he knew, but the loss was still fresh and living in his boyhood home made it harder to stay objective. Especially when the problem was a beautiful, naked female in his personal space.

Bandit tilted her tiny little head at him now and grinned like the know-it-all little female she was.

"Shut-up, Bandit. Stop looking at me like that." Yes, the

woman was breathtaking. Kissable. And that had *absolutely* nothing to do with his decision to talk to her before he turned her over to the cops.

Tim glanced in longing at the telephone one more time. *Therein lies the easy road.* And damned if he couldn't take it.

Some things never changed.

He rubbed the side of his neck in frustration. The skin itched and burned like he'd just been bitten by a fire-ant. Or electrocuted. Again. He walked to the kitchen area, stuck his neck under the faucet, and turned the cold water on as high as it would go. His hair had been kept regulation short for most of the last ten years. After the accident, he'd said to hell with it and just kept it shaved. He shoved his whole head under the cold water and tried to gain some damn perspective. The scar was almost a year old, but it still burned like hell once in a while. The docs called it Phantom Pain. Whatever. It burned on occasion, for no particular reason. This, apparently, was going to be one of those occasions.

Bandit barked and hopped up onto the couch, walking right on top of the woman and lying down on her torso like she had every right. Tim ignored her and stuck his neck back under the water, running possibilities through his mind. Gorgeous woman found naked in lake with no marks of any kind on her and seemingly in perfect health, except for the fact that she was unconscious. Oh, and she called him by name.

Coming up with a big fat zero on this one.

"Hi, baby."

Tim jerked at the soft voice, banging his head on the faucet and flinging water all over the counter and gray tile floor. He shut off the water and grabbed a hand towel, running it over his face, head, and neck.

"You're a cutie, aren't you?" The sing-song quality of the woman's voice filled his basement, unnaturally loud in the silence. Bandit's happy panting and snorting sounds carried to him as well. The little mutt was in doggie heaven.

Tim draped the towel around his shoulders to catch stray drops of water and slowly approached the couch. The pain in his neck had settled to a slow, steady burn, so he ignored it completely. He didn't want to scare the woman, but curiosity about her drove him forward. He realized it was genius to let the little fluff ball soften the woman up. Waking up to *him* might scare the shit out of her. He'd had grown men move across the street to avoid passing him on the sidewalk.

Idiots.

"Hi. How you feeling?" He stopped about ten feet away, then decided he'd better not stand over her like a towering giant if he wanted her to talk. He sank into one of the recliners, rested his forearms on his knees and laced his fingers together in front of him. No sudden moves, nothing to alarm her. He was not a small man. With his shaved head, tattoos, and scars, he knew he could be one mean looking son-of-a-bitch. And she was most likely a fairy-tale princess still looking for Prince Charming.

Even more irritating that the thought would bother him.

"Hi." She blinked up at him, but her right hand continued to rub his spoiled runt-dog's belly. "What day is it? How long was I gone?"

"It's Tuesday morning." Tim grabbed the towel off his shoulder and wiped a few stray drops of water off his forehead. "I pulled you out of Hendrick Lake about ten minutes ago."

She nodded, returning her attention to the dog.

"You're naked."

"He told me I would be." Not a trace of shock or teasing in her manner. She continued to snuggle with his traitorous little dog. "Thank you for getting me out of the water. It was freezing cold."

"You were unconscious."

"No. I've been aware the whole time. Watching. I had to wait for my energy to catch up in time."

What the hell was she talking about?

"It's okay about my hair. I appreciated the effort. And thank you for being such a gentleman." She sat up, tucking the blanket beneath her arms, showing a generous expanse of soft white skin and a long, elegant neck. The view was somehow more seductive now that the rest of her played peek-a-boo with his hungry eyes. Bandit growled a protest, then resettled on her lap. The woman laughed. Which was a good thing, because her preoccupation with the dog prevented her from seeing the red streaks he suspected were running up his neck to his ears.

She'd been *watching* him the whole time? *Listening to him?*

"Do you have some clothes I can borrow? We should really get going as soon as possible. They gave me the other Davis's address. But it's really her husband we need. He's the scientist. And we only have three days."

"Three days for what?"

She stared at him as if he had two heads. "To save Chicago." For the first time, he noticed her fingers shaking. Bandit whined and bumped her small head underneath the woman's palm. Her voice, when she continued, wavered a bit. "Didn't they tell you anything about the mission?"

The word 'mission' pounded through his skull like thunder and he jumped to his feet. "I'm out of that game, sweetheart. Whatever half-ass idea you've got brewing in your head, you better get rid of it now. I'm out and they damn well know it."

She bit her lip and stared, clearly at a loss, shaking and breathing more rapidly. Acting as if she were scared. He wasn't falling for it.

"Who are you? Who sent you? And how do you know my name?"

"The Archiver sent me to save Chicago. He gave me your name. He said you'd help me."

"I'm done with that. I don't save the world anymore." He walked around the coffee table and sat down on the thick oak inches away from her. He'd never heard the term 'Archiver' before, but it sounded just like something the feds would come up with. And sending her to tempt him? Brilliant. But no matter how enticing the bait, he wasn't hungry. "Why don't you call whoever sent you here and tell them to leave me out of it this time?"

Slowly, as if he were a Cobra about to strike, she lifted her hand and set her fingertips against the right side of his jaw. With a butterfly's touch she turned his face away so she could see his neck, where his skin continued to burn.

"But you have the mark." She placed cool fingers over the fiery area on his neck and held them there. Heat rolled through his neck and shoulder, like he'd just sunk into a warm bath. His whole body reacted to the sensation and he scowled at her.

"It's a burn scar, sweetheart."

"I see the scar. But the mark is there as well." Her dark hazel eyes rounded in empathy and shared pain.

Irritated at the pity in her eyes, the heat still flooding him, and the telltale bulge in his pants in reaction to it, he pulled from her grasp and marched to the small mirror hanging on the wall inside the tiny bathroom a few feet away. Turning his head to the side, he pulled on his neck, bringing his scar and the odd shape now imbedded within it into view in the mirror.

What the fuck was that?

Ω
Chapter Two

"Look. I have it, too."

He turned back at her softly spoken invitation, stunned to see a mark on the side of her neck that looked like an old hieroglyph in the rough shape of a circle, slightly open at the bottom, resting on a small line. It matched the new mark on his neck exactly. Same size. Same place...

"It's called a Shen. It's what they use to mark us when we are Taken and sent through time, and to mark those chosen to help us. My name is Sarah St. Pierre. You were chosen to help me, Timothy Daniel Tucker. The Archiver marked you."

"That's impossible." Tim shook his head, waiting for the next insane lie to fall from her lips. It wasn't the mark that he referred to. It was there, in his flesh. How and why he had no idea. No, it was her name that threw him for a loop. A name that made her a liar. Sarah St. Pierre was a name he knew, a name everyone who lived along any beach on Lake Michigan knew, a name a dozen different conspiracy theorists and cold case enthusiasts had romanticized over for a couple of decades or longer.

"Impossible or not, that's my name."

"How tall are you?"

"Six foot."

"What do you do for a living?"

"I was an Olympic athlete. Before I was Taken, I played professional beach volleyball and windsurfed in competitions. Why?"

Tim crossed his arms over his chest and studied her for several minutes. She didn't squirm, blink, or bat an eyelash at him. Her hazel green eyes, eyes that had won the hearts and souls of thousands of volleyball fans from the covers of sports magazines, stared straight into his. She appeared to utterly and completely believe what she was saying to him. She was tall. She had an athlete's body. She looked so very familiar. Still. "It's impossible."

"Why do you keep saying that?"

"Sweetheart, I don't know what kind of mind-game you are trying to pull, but Sarah St. Pierre is an urban legend. She disappeared more than twenty years ago. Working theory on her disappearance is that she was hit by lightning while windsurfing. Body never found. She's dead."

"No, I'm not."

"Don't move. I'll be right back." Tim raced upstairs to his old high-school bedroom, rifling through a complete collection of Sports Illustrated magazines in the trunk at the foot of his bed. His mother had never bothered to change his bedroom, and now that they were gone, he couldn't bring himself to change anything upstairs. But, on the good side, he knew exactly where to go to find the July 1987 issue. He remembered the date because his grandmother had lived in the town of Grand Haven the day of the freak storm. She'd even been interviewed by a national news station because her home lined the beach where Sarah St. Pierre's windsurfing board and sail had washed ashore…when he was seven years old.

He grabbed the magazine and ran back down the stairs. Then stopped in his tracks, frozen. There she was, on the cover.

Glancing from the magazine to the woman sitting on his couch and back, he walked up to her and held the photograph next to her face.

"What the f..." Perfect match, right down to the freckle at the corner of her left eye and the tiny scar centered under her perfectly pink lower lip. The quintessential, all-American, girl next door. Sunshine in a bottle.

She attempted a smile, but it didn't reach her eyes. "Told you so." She stood, and he couldn't help but notice that for once he faced an incredibly sexy woman whose lips were a scant few inches from his own. He wouldn't have to bend himself into a pretzel to kiss her.

Squeezing his hands into fists to resist the temptation of placing them on her warm, soft shoulders, he stared at her, a million questions rolling around inside his head. His mouth froze, incapable, for once, of asking any of them. Three days. Save Chicago. Missing woman arrives naked via lightning storm twenty-five years after her mysterious disappearance. Archiver. Shen. Scientist.

Shit. The fact that he was considering the possibility that any of this were true proved that he'd finally, completely lost his mind.

Inside his sick and twisted head he heard the theme music from the Mission Impossible movies cranking at top volume and then the voice... *Your mission, should you be crazy enough to accept it...*

All the while her eyes held him captive and the skin on

his scar burned anew, like someone had taken a branding iron to it in the *exact* shape of that strange mark beneath her ear.

Sarah studied the man before her and tried to reconcile what she'd been told with the fierce, hard-core, tough-as-nails ex-soldier who was supposed to help her. He wasn't soft. He didn't inspire thoughts of gentle wooing or sugar-coated realities. She couldn't imagine him running around at the beach playing volleyball and flirting with the over-exposed, overly-tanned, summer beach bunnies. He didn't fit in her sunny-side-up version of the world.

He was dark, brooding, and grumpy. Not at all what she had in mind for a husband. She'd always envisioned herself marrying a happy-go-lucky blond who loved to laugh, had a dimple in his cheek, and had an optimist's cheer always near the surface. She needed that light-heartedness.

She was dark. *She* was intense and competitive, always driven to do more, always waiting for the other shoe to drop, constantly fighting the fire in her gut pushing her on because, as a rule, people either disappointed her or died. Both outcomes hurt like hell, and she worked her butt off to make sure neither would permanently cripple her.

Now she had no choice. The newly shining mark of the Shen was still hot to the touch on his thickly corded neck. There wasn't an ounce of fat on him and he moved like a cagey predator, always watching his back, analyzing every sound. Constantly alert. That's how she would describe him. She doubted a spider could crawl across the floor even half a room away without him noticing it. Judging by the tense lines around his eyes, she doubted he slept much either.

He was a couple inches taller than she, which was saying

something. And he had to outweigh her by at least fifty pounds of rock solid chest and bulging muscles showcased to perfection by soft denim jeans and a snug, wet, molded-to-every-muscle, jersey cotton t-shirt. His head was shaved, and she guessed this chosen hairstyle had something to do with the jagged scar about three inches wide that began behind his right ear. The scar traveled down his head to curve around the side of his neck, cross his collarbone and disappear beneath his dark green t-shirt.

He'd been hurt at some point, burned. The thought didn't sit well with her and she found herself fighting the urge to trail her fingertips over the pale pink skin and trace it with her lips.

Once she'd explored there, she'd start on the tattoo playing peak-a-boo with her from beneath the shirt's collar on his right. If he'd had hair, it would probably be coffee colored to match the arrogant flare of his eyebrows. Startling gray eyes assessed her every move, studied her face. Stared at her lips. How utterly ridiculous that she would be hungering for a kiss, wondering how it would feel to be in his arms while he was most likely thinking of a hundred important, relevant, tactical questions that she couldn't answer.

Turning away from temptation, Sarah tried not to stare at everything around her, but it was all so strange. The Archiver had warned her that things had changed. She'd scoffed. How much could things really change in just a few years? But looking around Tim's basement at all the bizarre boxes, gadgets, and remote controls, she was out of her league and too exhausted at the moment to figure it all out.

Tim mumbled something about getting them both some dry clothes and disappeared up the stairs again, leaving her free to explore. She wrapped the blanket around herself as best she could and prayed her legs wouldn't collapse as she wandered toward the large black box hanging from the wall directly across from the couch. There were no buttons on the front, no numbers or any way to turn the thing on.

"That's the T.V." Tim spoke from behind her and she jumped at the sound of his voice.

"Where's the cable box? And the control panel?" Sarah ran her hands along the front of the smooth black frame. "How do you turn it on?"

"Well, it's hooked into the Internet through the gaming system right now." He lifted a remote control that looked like it could operate a spaceship and began pushing buttons. He might as well have been speaking Greek to her.

A large white screen appeared with a small rectangular box and colored letters. "Google?" Sarah turned to study the screen. "What is Google? Is that what T.V. is called now?"

"No." Tim grabbed a flat, black, shiny item and pushed another button. She moved closer. It looked like a tiny T.V. screen you could hold in your hands.

"What is that?"

"It's a tablet. An iPad."

"What does it do?"

"It's like a computer, only a lot smaller than the ones you probably remember."

Sarah narrowed her eyes as his fingers flew over the tablet and her name appeared in the box on the television. Then the T.V. screen changed and there were lists of things about her. Even some photos, career statistics, and several headlines about her disappearance.

"Newspapers are on television now?"

"Sort of. The Internet is hard to explain."

For the first time since she'd arrived her chest squeezed and the cold hand of doubt settled along her spine. Just a few years, but everything was different. Tim continued to flick fingers on the tablet and articles flashed on the screen, changing faster than she could read them. Photos of her, sun kissed and smiling with her fellow WPVA players and her old teammates from Pepperdine. Tim didn't give her time to read much, or reminisce about her old friends. She read headlines, scanned a sentence or two as quickly as she could manage. Then a photo of her grandmother appeared on the screen.

"Stop!"

Tim froze and she closed the distance until she stood inches from the giant photo of her beloved Granny T. It was an obituary. The old woman had apparently caused quite a stir, refusing to believe her granddaughter was dead and leaving everything she had in trust to a girl who'd been missing for over fifteen years. The article was dated 2003.

"She's gone."

"I'm sorry."

Sarah shook her head and refused to succumb to the burning behind her eyelids. Fingers shaking, she reached out to touch the smooth surface displaying the photo. "What year is it?" Energy crackled through her arm before a loud fizzing sound erupted from the black T.V. followed by a pop. The screen went black.

"2013." Tim pushed a few more buttons, then whispered under his breath. "And I think you just blew out my T.V., lightning girl."

"Twenty-five years." Gone. She leaned her forehead against the black screen in front of her, closing her eyes against the pain. If anyone had asked her a few minutes ago, she would have sworn she'd only spent a few hours in that odd laboratory with the Archiver, Celestina, and the terrifying visions of Chicago burning that had nearly driven her mad. Her friends would be old women now, grandmothers. Grandma Tilly was long gone, too. And the one thing she'd been so proud of, so sure would succeed, the Women's Professional Volleyball Association, had gone bankrupt after only a few years. "I don't think I like your Google."

Tim approached from behind her. From the corner of her eye she could see a pair of navy blue sweatpants, a navy and gold t-shirt with military insignia on it and a pair of rather large flip-flops in one of his hands. "Here. My mom was only five-two, so none of her stuff will fit you. I had to get out some of my old high-school stuff. Get dressed and then we'll figure it all out."

Sarah turned, but she didn't reach for the clothes. Instead, she walked straight into his chest, leaned her head against his shoulder, and prayed she wouldn't have to beg for the hug she desperately needed. The Archiver told her this man would help her, protect her, and fight at her side when the time came to battle the silver snowflakes of doom. Celestina, the Seer, swore to her that she could trust the man, no matter how rugged or gruff he seemed. He looked more like a biker than the boy-next-door type she was used to. Hugging hadn't specifically been listed in his job description, but Tim didn't know that and she wasn't about to enlighten him as his thickly muscled arms finally wrapped around her bare shoulders and snugged her in close to his large body.

She relaxed against him, inhaling his rugged scent, and jumped right off the cliff.

"I need you to take me to Luke Lawson. 1339 Valley

Court in Bannockburn. He's the scientist I told you about. I need him. And we have to go today."

I need him. Sarah's hot breath pushed the words through the soft cotton of his t-shirt and his arms tensed. He didn't like hearing her claim to need another man. It was insane. It was stupid. It was gut fucking instinct. And like it or not, he was going to help her any way he could so he could continue to look himself in the mirror each morning.

"Okay. Let's eat breakfast, and then I'll drive you wherever you need to go." She shuddered in his arms and nodded into his neck. Inexplicably, she wrapped her arms around his waist and squeezed. Unable to resist the sweet seduction of her bare shoulders another minute, he lifted his palm to her back and brushed his fingers beneath her hair and along her spine in what he hoped were soothing strokes. The wet heat of tears soaked his neck and the collar of his shirt for several minutes before she whispered a reply.

"Thank you."

She pulled out of his arms and he would've sworn the temperature in the room plummeted fifteen degrees. Suddenly, he didn't know where to put his hands so he pointed back to the small bathroom. "I'll make breakfast. Shower's through there. You might want to use it. You smell like lake moss and dead fish."

She grinned and grabbed the clothing he'd brought down for her. "Could be worse, I guess."

"Could be." *Lie. Lie. Lie.* She smelled like heaven on earth and the caveman inside of him wanted to drag her into his bedroom, tug the blanket out of her hands, and spend the whole afternoon exploring every inch of her delectable body. But she wanted to go see another man, a scientist in

Bannockburn. He'd rather lock her in his bedroom and ravage her until all thought fled from her lightning quick mind, but he'd have to be dead before he'd admit it aloud.

She closed the bathroom door behind her and the spell was broken. He shifted the uncomfortable bulge in his pants around and frowned. He must be going crazy. He'd known the woman for all of an hour! And Bannockburn?

Whatever. He'd make eggs, then drive her to see her precious scientist in rich-man's-land. After that…well, she wouldn't be his responsibility anymore, would she?

Bandit growled at him from her cozy bed next to the unlit fireplace, then yapped out two short barks that sounded suspiciously like, 'Yeah, right.'

"Shut-up, dog." He growled at Bandit, who rolled over for a belly-rub in response. Spoiled little rat. He leaned down to oblige the little rodent, but the moment didn't last long.

The soft click of the bathroom door's latch preceded a soft, sharp whistle. Bandit's ears popped up and she jumped out of bed. Her tail wagged so fiercely it looked like the little puff-ball was going to fall over laughing at him as she sauntered toward the bathroom to join her new best friend in the shower. Hot water. Soap. Lots and lots of bare skin.

The door closed once again behind the little traitor and he heard Sarah's soft laughter. Now he was jealous of a ten pound fur-ball that smelled like dead fish.

Tim started cooking and let his mind work on the problem at hand. It was either that or stare at the bathroom door like a lust-filled fifteen year old boy. By Sarah's account he had a time-traveler to deliver to a man in Bannockburn. But he knew it was more than that. Much more.

He'd missed something. Someone had continued his

research. He'd do whatever he had to do to stop them, even play along with the gorgeous liar in his bathroom until she led him back to the enemy's lair.

Ω

Chapter Three

Tuesday, 11:00 AM

Tim kept his eyes on the highway, safely averted from the woman to his right. Bandit lay curled up in her lap, still shivering from her bath, but smelling much better. Sarah absently stroked the soft hair on the top of Bandit's head and stared straight ahead. She looked like a lost doll with eyes too big for her face. She'd supposedly been gone, absent, missing for over twenty years and she didn't crane her neck in curiosity once? It was almost like she was afraid to look outside.

"We should be there in about thirty minutes."

"That's fine." Sarah closed her eyes and let her head fall back against the headrest. "Luke probably won't be home yet, anyway. Hopefully, Alexa will be there. Maybe she can help us."

A half hour later, Tim squeezed the steering wheel until his knuckles were white. He'd asked for answers at breakfast, but all she'd told him was that it was complicated and she didn't want to have to explain it twice. She'd asked him to wait until they reached this scientist's house. He'd tried to be patient, he really had. But the soldier in him was used to recon and planning, not trusting a doe-eyed female to tell him what to do and where to go when lives were on the line. And if his suspicions were correct, a lot of lives were at stake. All his fault. It made his stomach curl and head ache.

He forced his fingers to loosen their death grip. Thirty minutes of silence was all he could take. He'd thought Sarah would crack, ramble on like a typical female, like his mother would have with her incessant chatter. But no. He had to meet the only woman on the planet who talked less than he did. Which meant, if he wanted answers, he was going to have to drag them out of her.

Sure, she'd asked him to wait. Sarah wanted to share her secrets with someone else. Luke. The scientist who had more than likely stolen his work. Tim was ready to strangle the jerk and he hadn't even met him. They were less than three blocks from the bastard's house and he couldn't stop himself from casing the neighborhood. He would not go in blind.

Gun loaded. Check. Knife. Check. She claimed she had no idea where they were going. If he spent some extra time doing recon and making sure Google Maps had their shit together with this neighborhood, she'd never know the difference. He'd map the exits before he put them both in danger.

Then he'd be able to breathe.

Even if every other breath crippled him because his traitorous nose did nothing but zero in on the smell of her sweet skin beneath his glycerin soap. The recon might take a bit longer than usual, since he was obviously operating with half a brain, and had been since pulling her out of the water.

Losing brain cells over a woman's scent wasn't something he'd ever experienced before. He couldn't imagine the effect being any worse on his thinking skills if he were mainlining heroin.

He wanted her. And he didn't want anything. Ever. He didn't need that kind of distraction now, couldn't afford it. Of course, if that had been part of their plan, it was working like a charm.

Biggest problem with the whole thing? That new mark on his neck. That screwed every theory he had. It's not like they'd sneaked in and tattooed him with burning ink...

"We've driven past the house twice now, you know." Sarah stared out the window as she spoke, her long elegant fingers stroking Bandits small head.

And he didn't think she'd been paying attention. Guess she wasn't as unnerved by his oh-so-manly combination of Old Spice antiperspirant, lake water, and wet dog.

"Give me a few minutes to check things out."

"Okay." Sarah stared at him for a moment and Tim felt like a frog under a microscope. She knew what he was doing. The knowledge shined out of her eyes. She knew, she understood, and apparently, she agreed that it was necessary.

That worried him. What the hell was he getting himself into? And why couldn't he walk away? God knew this whole scenario screamed nothing but trouble.

"If you want my help, you've got to start talking to me. You can start by telling me where you've been all these years and why you haven't aged a single day." Tim gritted his teeth so hard his jaw ached and went back to checking rooflines, corners, cars, and shadows. He'd probably crack a damn tooth, but he'd wait her out, get some answers.

All the while, that mark on the side of his neck heated and burned, like he'd been injected with a twelve hour Bengay time-capsule under the skin. His scar was normally numb, so the extra sensation was making him edgy.

She sighed, and Bandit lifted her head to glare at him when Sarah's fingers stopped moving in her fur yet again. "Your Google was right. I was wind-surfing that day. I did get struck by lightning. But what it doesn't know is that it wasn't just a freak storm that blew in over Lake Michigan." Sarah took a deep breath and rubbed Bandit's ears. "In fact, I'm not sure what it was. All I know is I was surfing, then sizzling, then I spent what felt like a few hours in a strange room hallucinating..." A shudder raced through her shoulders and Tim resisted the urge to remove his hand from the steering wheel so he could run his fingers under her hair and rub the tension out of her neck muscles.

"You still haven't answered my questions. Where were you?"

Sarah's silence felt like it dragged on for a week. "Even if I tell you now, you won't believe me. Not until you meet Alexa and Luke."

He wanted to push her but he was afraid she was right. "Then tell me something I will believe."

"Friday morning, at dawn, Chicago is going to be attacked by an advanced weapons system that uses some kind of freak ionic particles. All of Chicago, every building, every person, *everything* is going to be incinerated in a matter of minutes."

Nine million people. *Ionic weapon.* Tim's instincts roared to life. Those bastards couldn't have completed the weapon without him. He'd destroyed everything, all of his research, every file replaced with useless and complex drivel, every hard drive scrambled, every piece of paper shredded and imposters put into play. He would not be another Leo Szilard.

Point him in the right direction and he'd kill the bastards before they got the attack off the ground. He had friends who'd help. Couple phone calls and he'd have a team of guys ready to roll in less than twelve hours, guys who knew how to take care of things. "Who has it? Where are they? And why did you show up in my back yard?"

"I don't know who they are or why. The Archiver didn't tell me that. I'm not sure even they know. The CIA, FBI, police, military, none of them would believe me. You know that. They'd throw me in a dark hole somewhere and write me off as insane. Then Chicago would burn and they'd torture me for information I can't give them. And it will happen. They can't stop it. I'm the only one who can stop it and Celestina said I need your help to do it."

"What, exactly, do you need me to do?"

"I don't know for sure. But we need to find their ship before they attack. And if we can't find it, we'll need a plan to deactivate the particles somehow once the attack begins. We have to figure out how to neutralize them, or redirect the charge. I honestly don't know."

"You said a ship? Like what, a stealth bomber? Military jet?"

"No. More advanced. A spaceship from another time."

"Bullshit, Sarah." Good grief, the woman had him going there for a minute.

"Why? Because it's a U.F.O. or because I said it's not from this time?"

"Both."

"Yeah, well the joke's on you then. You're sitting next to a woman who died twenty-five years ago. If you can buy that, it's not much of a stretch to think other people would be able to use the same time warping technology." Bandit danced on her lap in annoyance as the tension mounted in the truck cab. With a sigh, Sarah settled her shoulders and released a long, slow breath before continuing. Tim bit his tongue, and waited for the next fantastic tale to fall from those perfect pink lips.

"I was told that the bad guys are from the future. That's why they have the advanced weaponry. The Archiver said they've been here trying to find these guys and stop them for over a thousand years." Without warning, Sarah reached across the console between them and touched the mark burning on his neck. "That's the symbol of the Timewalkers. We're chosen, Taken, then marked by the Archiver and his crew."

"So, you were gone for twenty-five years because you were traveling through time. And you were recruited by other time travelers, in a spaceship, who've been here for over a thousand years?"

"Yes."

Assuming he could swallow that tall tale…"How are you supposed to redirect the charge of this weapon if it's big enough to take out all of Chicago?"

"They did something to me on the ship, after I'd been hit by the lightning. I can feel electricity now, kinetic energy, all energy. Everywhere. I've got to find a way to change the charge. Or absorb it. Something. I don't know. That's why I need help."

"So, you don't know how you're supposed to pull off this miracle?"

"No. I have ideas, but I won't really know what I'm facing until we're under attack."

"We have less than seventy-two hours to come up with a plan? And you'll have a matter of minutes to stop it? Then everything burns?"

"Right."

"Ionic particles? Electromagnetic particles? Dark matter? Geothermal? Solar? What are we dealing with, exactly?"

"Don't know. But it incinerates everything it touches in seconds."

"And you want me to help you battle these mystery particles from a futuristic weapon while we're in the middle of an attack by a hostile alien spaceship?" If it weren't so ludicrous, he'd be laughing out loud. Well, that and the serious, haunted expression of the woman next to him, the woman who'd traveled through time and dropped into the lake, naked, next to his boat just this morning.

"Yes. I'm sorry. I hoped the Archiver would've told you about this before my arrival." A tear tracked down her cheek and she hastily wiped it away before squaring her shoulders. "This is why I need Luke. I always loved art and reading, but stunk at math. He's a scientist and can explain this stuff better than I can. He'll help you understand."

"I doubt it, but we're about to find out."

It was like a dam had burst. Now that Sarah was talking, she appeared to be unable to stop. "Alexa is from another time as well. She just arrived here about a month ago for her mission. Celestina said it's odd that another attack is happening so soon. The Triscani usually wait longer." There was an edge to Sarah's voice he didn't like, a tight, clipped quality to her words that he only heard when a woman was enraged or in deep pain. Hell if he knew which one it was.

"Who are the Triscani?"

"The bad guys. I don't know much about them. I just know that the Archiver followed them here. They're from the future, too."

"So, every few years this Archiver guy grabs a woman who was supposed to die, takes her up into his fancy spaceship, that's from the future, and sends her through time to battle hostile aliens?" He tried to keep his voice even. He really did, but knew she'd heard the doubt in his tone.

"I know it sounds crazy. I'm sorry. Just wait until you meet Alexa and Luke."

Tim pulled into the driveway but didn't kill the engine. Sure, Sarah was here, in his time, and not dead. That was weird. But how did he know she was really who she said she was? Plastic surgery and a twenty-five year old photograph wouldn't be too hard to fake these days. The assholes he used to work for would stoop lower than that if they thought it would get them what they wanted. Throwing this tall, sexy female at him was one of their more brilliant options. In fact, he'd bet his ass this Luke fellow worked for the same set of assholes he used to. The whole thing screamed set-up. However, his bullshit detector, usually rock solid and always on, was strangely silent. Why? Nothing added up.

"This is insane." Tim didn't mean to insult the woman, but what the hell was he supposed to think? An electromagnetic weapon like she described would mean certain death for a hell of a lot of people. The swing in world power, politics, and war would be on a scale similar to the shift in power after the bombing of Hiroshima when nuclear power entered the fray.

An attack on the scale she was talking about? Millions of lives, billions of dollars in damage to the city? The whole country, hell, the whole world, would panic. Chicago was a financial mega-city second only to New York in big money and big players. No one in their right mind would try to control that kind of energy with hocus-pocus. If someone had actually built that kind of weapon...

"Yes, it is insane. But if I don't find a way to stop it, all of this," she waved her hand in the air to encompass the city surrounding them. "*All of this*, and all the people are going to be incinerated in three days. That's why we have to find their ship before Friday. I'd rather take them out before they attack. The odds of survival seem much higher."

"No kidding." He could call in some favors and get a team together, but the guys would either fall over laughing, or ask him if he'd lost his mind. Probably both.

"I told you that you wouldn't believe me." Sarah turned to face him and he no longer had the pull of the road to keep his gaze from an intense perusal of her sad, stubborn face.

"I guess you were right." Their eyes locked, and it was all he could do not to move forward. He stopped thinking at all, like she hypnotized him or telepathically controlled his mind and desires. He used to laugh at the weak-willed human that was seduced and controlled by a vampire on the television shows he occasionally watched. True Blood on DVD had become his guilty pleasure. Something about seeing those primal fuckers wreak havoc on the world appealed to him. No weakness tolerated. No bullshit. Just blood, will, and survival of the fittest.

With Sarah, it seemed she was the hunter and he the prey.

So not going to happen.

Tim turned away from her and broke the spell just as Bandit growled and jumped to her feet, hopping back and forth from Sarah's window to his as he finally killed the engine in the driveway of an impressive two-story colonial style home. White house. Blue shudders. Red door surrounded by roses and expertly manicured shrubs beneath giant oak trees. An American flag hung prominently from a post next to the door. The whole place was picture perfect. It looked like the photo from a Christmas card, without the colored lights.

Then the front door opened and a giant yellow lab raced to Sarah's window, barking happily at Bandit's supercharged growl. His vicious runt of a dog wagged her tail as fast as it would go and plastered her face against the window, covering it in dog snot.

If nothing else came of this, at least Bandit was happy. Small consolation, but he'd take what he could get.

Sarah's hand closed around her door handle and he reached over her legs to cover her hand with his before she could open the door. "Don't."

"He looks friendly."

"Let me go first. I don't know these people. I don't trust them."

She actually rolled her eyes at him, but she sat back and waved at his door with her free hand. "Go ahead."

Surprised at his reluctance to let go of her hand, he slowly pulled back and opened his door. As he walked around the hood to meet the yellow lab a woman emerged from the house. Tiny thing. Five foot two at most, maybe a hundred pounds, with hair that was so blond it looked silver hanging to her waist. A welcoming smile reached all the way to her blue eyes. She was gorgeous and covered the distance with a bounce in her step. She wore a deep blue tank top and white capris with gem-studded flip-flops. Not much space to hide a weapon. Tim relaxed a fraction.

"Hi. You must be Timothy."

The muscles in his shoulders squeezed tight again. How the hell did she know that?

Behind him, the truck's passenger door opened and Sarah's long legs slid into view, followed by her lithe body. His baggy sweatpants did nothing to hide her natural strength or grace. Sarah stepped forward until the two women stood within arm's reach. She towered over their tiny host by nearly a foot, like a golden goddess looking down on a silver fairy. "Are you Alexa?"

"I am." Alexa walked forward and held out her hand. "You must be Sarah."

Sarah nodded and shook the smaller woman's hand while Bandit and the big dog said 'Hello' to each other in the usual nose-in-personal-places method. Tim scanned the rooftops and moved closer to Sarah, in case there was trouble. "We should get inside."

The women ignored him.

"How did you know we were coming?" Sarah scooped Bandit into her arms and cradled the dog against her shoulder.

"The Archiver." Silence descended while Alexa stared at the two of them in turn. Was it his imagination, or did Alexa relax a bit after searching out the matching marks on their necks? "Luke will be here any minute. Please, come in. The Archiver wouldn't tell Luke anything, but I know if you're here it can't be good."

"That's an understatement." Sarah sighed. She and Alexa looked at each other again, a sadness hanging in the air between them that he didn't understand.

"Yes. I'm sure it is." There wasn't a hint of humor in Alexa's voice or a second's reprieve from the melancholy look in her eyes as she watched them both. "How much time do you have?"

"Friday at sunrise."

"Planet wide?"

"Just Chicago."

Alexa nodded stoically and led them into the house, not a hint of doubt, disbelief, or question in her eyes. Instead, Tim saw understanding, empathy, and a healthy dose of fear in the tense lines around Alexa's eyes and mouth.

Both women looked like they were facing a firing squad. Either they were both insane, or they both believed what they were saying. Didn't matter because he couldn't do a thing about it.

Despite his desire to stay out of the soap opera, seeing the ladies' obvious upset made him want to destroy something…even if it were a time-traveling alien's spaceship. Hoo-Rah.

***

"Why Chicago?" Luke Lawson entwined his fingers with Alexa's where they met midair between the two chairs and set his coffee cup down on the antique oak coffee table. Tim knew quality when he saw it, and they were all sitting on about forty thousand dollars' worth of wood. What a waste of money. But he had his back to the wall, Sarah sitting next to him on the sofa, a clear view of all the windows, and three people surrounding him who believed every word they were saying.

He'd patiently listened and waited while Sarah told them the same story she'd thrown at him in the car. Advanced weapon. Spaceship. Electromagnetic attack. Chicago gone.

They didn't even blink.

And he thought his day couldn't get any weirder.

"The Archiver and Celestina don't know why. Their enemies have never targeted a specific city before, or attacked again so soon."

"Who's Celestina?" Alexa leaned forward in her chair and focused her intense glacier blue eyes on Sarah.

"The Seer. She is the one who sees all the attacks and tells the Archiver to find one of us. Didn't you meet her when they sent you?" Sarah looked confused, her shoulders and lips tensing in alarm.

"I never met anyone but the Archiver. And he didn't tell me half of what he's told you. He didn't tell my mother, either. And she was a Walker before me. I knew what I had to do, that's it." Alexa gestured at Tim in apparent irritation. "I didn't know who my marked mate would be."

Tim frowned as his brain analyzed and processed everything they'd said, everything but one. "Did you say mate?" Sure, Sarah was attractive, and roused all of his instincts, but mate?

Sarah ignored him completely and Alexa talked over the top of him. "I didn't know the release of the Red Death was orchestrated by aliens from another time. They didn't dump me in Luke's lap like a gift-wrapped present. Why didn't they tell me any of this?"

"I don't know." Sarah shrugged and moved away from him in a small retreat of crossed legs and shifting hips. She hadn't looked at him once since they'd all sat down. He didn't like it. "My understanding is that Celestina sees what they are going to do, and then the Archiver grabs one of us to try to fix it."

"Did they tell you how many of us there are?"

Sarah shook her head. "No. But I kinda got the impression there have been a lot. He did say they've been battling these guys, trying to figure out what they want, for about a thousand years."

"An attack every few years, for a thousand years?" Luke whistled low and shook his head. "That would be hundreds of Timewalkers, plus all their descendants."

Luke looked between him and Sarah as the silence stretched across the table and became a chasm in the small space between his shoulder and Sarah's. Alexa studied her fingernails and Sarah studied the wood swirls in the table as a pink flush crept into her cheeks. Luke grinned. "He doesn't know?"

Ω
Chapter Four

Sarah glanced at him quickly, like a moth dancing in and out of a flame. "I just met him a few hours ago."

Luke's hands sought the buttons on his white oxford shirt. In a few quick flicks of his fingers he'd removed it, then tugged at his white undershirt until he pulled it over his head.

Tim stared. Sure, the guy was in decent shape, but that wasn't what drew his eyes. He ignored the bullet wound on the guy's side. Unusual for a civilian, but easily dismissed when the real reason Luke had disrobed was so clearly on display. There, over his left pec, right above his heart, was a mark exactly like the one Sarah had on her neck, the same symbol he now had on his. His mark chose that moment to flare up and tingle like an army of tiny popsicles were racing under his skin.

The mark on Luke's chest shocked him. The overload of feeling in his long-numbed out scar mocked his logic and rocked reality beneath him. And the physical sensations, the burning heat, continued to get stronger.

Luke pointed to his own neck, to the space where Tim had been marked. "You're hers and she's yours. You better come to grips with that fast or you two won't survive."

The words didn't have time to sink in before Luke asked another question he couldn't answer. "What's your gift? How are you linked? Have you figured it out yet?"

Sarah looked as confused as he felt. Alexa sighed and shook her head with a sad smile. "You'll figure it out when you need to."

"What was yours?" Tim met Luke's gaze, unflinching. Science geek? Super nerd? Ripped abs and a recent bullet wound? This guy was not what he'd expected.

"I can sense Alexa's presence and track her anywhere in the world. It was a skill I needed to save her life. The Archiver will have given you a link to Sarah, something you will need to master to help her."

Sarah wouldn't look at him.

"I'm nothing special. I'm a pilot. Not some kind of superhero with special powers." Tim tried to make them see reason.

Alexa shook her head. "Those are skills you already had, just like Luke knew about the virus and how to deal with it."

"I've studied phsyics." An understatement, but he couldn't resist throwing out the bait, see if Luke bit. He didn't.

Luke shook his head. "It's not enough. The Archiver chose you for a specific reason. Do you have any kind of E.S.P.? You know, telepathy or clairvoyance? Something really unusual?"

Tim raised an eyebrow and buried the flash of disappointment and disgust deep. He'd been really close to believing the whole thing. But this hit too close to home. What did Luke know? What did Sarah know?

He studied Sarah's profile, thoughts reeling. Electromagentics. Advanced weaponry. *His* research. *Oh, and by the way Tim, are you psychic?*

Yes, this 'Archiver' person knew just what to throw in his path, just the bait to use, to draw him in. Someone had gotten their hands on his research all right, and his military records. Now he had to stick around so he could find them and eliminate them.

The tingling in his neck amped up another notch as Sarah wrung her hands in her lap, twisting them until the fingertips were stark white.

The hanging light flickered then popped above their heads. Sarah flinched.

"Sorry."

Alexa looked from him to Sarah. "You can't control it?"

Sarah shook her head, her lost expression darting between the mark seared into Luke's chest and his hand, wrapped around Alexa's. "Not all the time."

Tim leaned forward. "First, put your shirt back on, champ." Sarah looked at him, a question in her eyes. "Assuming you three aren't out of your minds, then there is a significant threat out there that we need to eliminate. And that threat is coming from the air."

Sarah nodded.

"Sarah, you told me you could feel energy, could possibly find their ship."

"Yes, I believe so."

"Then we need to get you into the air. I'm not flying my chopper with bottled lightning on board. Too dangerous. But we need to get to high ground. And nowhere is higher around here than the Skydeck at Willis Tower, or the Hancock Observatory."

Luke nodded in agreement. "The Hancock Observatory isn't quite as tall, but it's got giant broadcasting antennae on its roof and it's closer to the water. It'll give you a great view of the city and the lake, and it's not quite as busy with tourists."

Sarah put her hands in her lap and stared him straight in the eye "Hancock then, if it's closer to the water. The attack is going to come in from the north, over the lake. At least, that's how it happened in my visions." The defiant tilt of her chin dared Tim to doubt her.

He didn't doubt she'd had a vision. That was one area in which he had firsthand experience. Bu these people didn't need to know that just yet. "Let's go."

"You two aren't quite ready for that." Luke leaned back in his seat, shirt back on. Thank God, because Tim really didn't want to have to hurt him.

"Do you have a better idea?" Sarah closed her eyes, and Tim noticed the dark circles beneath them, the way she suddenly swayed in her chair. The mark on his neck zinged with new life right before the whole house buzzed with an electrical surge. The microwave popped in the kitchen behind them and the refrigerator kicked off, then back on.

"You've got to learn control, Sarah. And I think Tim is the key."

"What?" Tim rubbed his scar absently.

"You grimaced before each of her power surges. You could feel the power building in your Shen, couldn't you?"

Tim thought about it for a second. The first time it had acted up was right before she'd blown up his T.V. Then he'd been in a constant state of buzzing pain until she blew the light and now the fridge. "Yes."

"You have to help her control it. I don't know how, but you two need to figure out how to work together."

Alexa studied him for a moment and broached a subject no one had dared in months. "Your scar, it's an electrical burn, isn't it?"

Sarah gasped and Tim nodded.

"Now it all makes perfect sense." Luke chimed in, then got up and walked around to stand behind his wife's chair.

"Not to me. Why did we need to come here? I would have helped Sarah without your involvement." Tim rubbed his neck in an attempt to stop the buzzing pain.

"Would you?" Luke studied him like he was a rat under a microscope, like a disapproving father inspecting the horny teenage boy picking up his daughter for the prom.

"Yes." He would have. Despite his grumbling, he realized he couldn't have walked away no matter how crazy Sarah had sounded. He could rationalize it all he wanted. He had a responsibility to make sure his work didn't ever reach fruition in the world. But a deeper, more primal part of him admitted that it simply wasn't in him to leave a damsel in distress. Especially one so...tired. God, she looked like she was going to drop right there onto the coffee table.

"Good." Luke's hands caressed his wife's shoulders as naturally as he was breathing. Tim looked away.

"I can help you two. You can use an insulated room at Fermilab to get a handle on her power. Alexa and I can sneak you in tonight. There's plenty of electricity and no one will notice big spikes in power out there."

"I thought the particle accelerator was shut down." Tim was far from surprised.

"That's the official story."

Tim didn't like the sound of this at all. Sneaking onto a government run top-secret testing facility with two women, one of whom was a six-foot tall, drop dead gorgeous female who had disappeared over twenty years ago. Hell, yeah. That would go over well.

"I don't need to do that." Sarah chimed in. "I can feel more than enough power now. The city's electrical grid, even the movement of the air in the room, everything feeds me power if I want it. I don't need a power source."

Alexa's eyes widened in shock. "Wow. You're serious, aren't you?"

"As a heart attack." Sarah crossed her arms over her chest and leaned back into the sofa when Alexa sat back in alarm, fear widening her eyes for the first time.

Tim changed the subject. "Let's hit the Hancock Observatory tonight, after it's closed, and see what Sarah can do from there." He glanced at Sarah, who nodded in agreement before continuing, "I just don't know how we're going to get in without being on a hundred security cameras and setting off alarms. I'm sure they don't welcome overnight guests. Plus, we'll need some privacy."

"Got it covered." Alexa laughed, then squeezed Luke's hand. Smiling like a couple of Cheshire cats, they vanished into thin air.

Tim shot to his feet and had Sarah wedged behind him before he registered her delighted laugh. She patted him on the shoulder and tried to wiggle free.

"It's okay, Tim." She left her hand on his shoulder and he relaxed enough to let her breathe, but blocked her when she attempted to squeeze out into the open. Her warm breath tickled his cheek as she beamed over his shoulder at the now empty space. "Lexa, that was awesome!"

"I've been practicing." The voice came from nowhere,

and Tim left his hand on his knife, just in case.

"Don't kill them, soldier. Invisibility is her gift."

Luke and Alexa reappeared as if by magic. Alexa's smile was irresistible, so Tim grinned back.

"Handy." It would have saved his ass a lot of trouble on more than one occasion in the field. Maybe that explained the calls to his unit commander. Had they been trying to recruit him into some sort of specialized unit? Or were Alexa, Luke, and Sarah for real and Chicago's nine million residents in grave danger?

Luke grinned and kissed his wife full on the mouth. "Yes, and it's how we're going to get to the top of the observatory tonight." Luke's attention shifted away from his wife to the two of them. "Stay here for a couple hours. Rest. Eat. We'll leave at eighteen-hundred hours."

Just like that he was committed hook, line and sinker.

Sarah wrapped her arms around her middle as Alexa chipped in, "We'll stop and get you some clothes, Sarah. And shoes that fit you."

Tim shook his head. World ending disasters afoot, leave it to a woman to worry about clothes.

Luke pulled Alexa to her feet and wrapped his arm around her waist. "There's a storm blowing in tonight. Sarah, you look like you could use some rest. I'll do some research on what kind of weapon you could be dealing with. Then we'll head over to the Hancock Observatory and see if Sarah can ride the lightning." Luke's pathetic joke did nothing to ease Tim's mind.

They needed a game plan. In the field he'd excelled at analyzing the opposition, the mission. Strengths. Weaknesses. Even personalities of all the players, who they could ice and whose cage they could rattle enough to give up Intel. Who they could use, and who they'd have to eliminate.

But this time he had no clear enemy. No information. And no control over her game. That was the most frustrating thing of all. He wasn't used to being out of control, in any way. And now? He sat next to a woman who couldn't sneeze without potentially blowing something up.

And he was more convinced than ever that someone had stolen his work. Even if that weren't the case, and these 'aliens from the future' were for real, who better to understand their technology? He'd been on the brink of creating that kind of device himself. That's why he'd corrupted his own work and destroyed the rest. This kind of thing shouldn't even be possible. Some things humanity should just leave alone.

Nine million people needed him to figure this out. Fast. And all Sarah could do at the moment was stare blankly at a whorl of stained wood in front of her and hold back tears. It looked like she could barely move, let alone come up with a plan of attack.

She was an asset, a weapon. A piece on the chessboard he needed to learn how to play. At the moment, she wasn't much better than a mannequin with red rimmed, glassy eyes, lead-filled limbs, and a vacant, frozen face.

She looked both exhausted and scared to death.

Not sure if the overture would be welcome, he placed his hand gently over hers where it rested in a fist against her thigh.

Sarah sighed, and the mark on the side of his neck went oddly numb. After the constant tingling and humming beneath his scar, the sudden lack of sensation left him empty.

"I was afraid of that." Alexa's whispered words echoed in the eerily silent room. She nodded her head in Sarah's direction. Sarah's head had fallen to the side in an awkward angle wedged against the back of the couch, asleep. "When was the last time she slept?"

Tim shrugged. "I have no idea. She was unconscious this morning for about fifteen minutes when I pulled her out of the lake."

"How long since she'd rested before that?" Alexa shifted and looked directly at him without blinking. "The energy won't let her rest unless you're there to ground her."

Tim glanced down at his hand where it rested over Sarah's lightly freckled skin, then back up at the oh-so-serious couple staring at him like he was their pet project.

"You can't leave her side until she learns what this is going to do to her, until she learns some control. It'll be too dangerous for everyone." Luke's warning sank in and he imagined the worst. Apparently, Alexa did, too, because it looked like the little woman was on the verge of tears.

"All right." Tim looked back at Sarah. It's not like touching her was a big sacrifice. He knew exhaustion when he saw it. Sarah had literally passed out. He'd been too distracted, too caught up in his own thoughts to notice the sunken look of her eyes or the pale tone of her skin. It didn't matter much to him whether she was a pawn or a queen. She was a vital piece of the puzzle he needed to solve. He needed to keep her close until he did.

Careful not to break contact with her, Tim slid his arms beneath her willowy body and lifted her from the chair. "Got somewhere she can rest for a few hours?"

"Of course." Alexa moved around her husband to lead

him down a hallway off the kitchen.

"What time is the storm supposed to hit tonight?"

Luke checked his watch. "In about seven hours. The Observatory closes at eleven. We should be there by ten to make sure they'll sell us a ticket. Alexa can hide us and Sarah can zap the cameras after they shut the place down for the night." Luke stared at his wife. "And then we're leaving town."

Tim agreed. Assuming Chicago was not a safe place to be right now, if it were his wife, they'd already be halfway to California.

Tim studied the light dusting of freckles on Sarah's innocent but determined face. She looked like she worried, even in her sleep. She should be on a beach drinking margaritas and getting a suntan.

Nothing new for him here. Lies. Deceit. Danger. He'd lived this life for years. It might drive him insane to think about dragging a helpless woman into a fight, but he'd do it. It went against every instinct he had, made the muscles in his back and neck so tight he felt like a guitar string about to snap, but he'd do what needed to be done.

"We'll be ready."

* * *

Before she opened her eyes, Sarah knew two things. One, the constant buzzing pain was gone. And two, she was draped all over the left side of one sexy-as-hell soldier who had said the word 'mate' like it was cancer.

She'd just met the man. His distrust and cold rejection shouldn't hurt, but they did. She was still the too-tall, too-skinny, freckle-faced freak who couldn't get a date to the prom.

Echoes of a thousand thoughtless comments filled her mind. 'How's the weather up there?' 'I sure hope you play basketball.' And her favorite, 'Don't step on us little people.'

No man had dared kiss her until she was nearly twenty-one. And he'd been a hotshot basketball star at Purdue, convinced he was God's gift to women, and disgusted by the fact that she refused to drop her pants and beg for his less-than-noble intentions on the first date. Hell, the first hour of their first date.

Her experience with men, other than her father, had been that they were either intimidated as hell by her six-foot frame, or wanted to sleep with her so they could brag about the novelty to their friends.

Tim's arm was draped across her waist, and he was dead asleep lying on his side beside her. Just holding her.

She hadn't felt this safe since the car accident when she was seven and her big brother, Nathan, had rocked her to sleep in her grandmother's recliner, both of them crying. That was the day they'd lost their parents. But it was her big brother, and she trusted him completely. Four years later he'd left for some secret mission in the South American jungle and never come home.

Now she'd lost over twenty years. Her friends. Her career. Her grandmother. She'd been promised a man who would love her forever. Instead she got a twitchy, tattooed, ex-military hard-ass who treated her with kid gloves and looked at her like she was his tenth grade science assignment, a frog in need of dissection. A puzzle that needed to be solved.

A weapon to be deployed. It had almost been easier

when he hadn't believed her, when she'd just been a naked woman dropped like an orphaned baby on his doorstep. When she hadn't craved his touch or his approval. When he'd been a faceless possibility, a romantic dream. When she'd been stupid enough to believe the Archiver when he told her it would all work out.

Maybe that super-psychic jerk had his own special blend of happy gas on that stupid spaceship of his. The whole thing had sounded like a grand adventure to her then. She'd zapped spheres and shot electrical bolts from her fingertips with ease.

Small fry, she now realized, to shooting lightning over the entire Chicago skyline or figuring out how to defeat an advanced alien weapon *on the fly.*

A softly ticking pendulum clock on the wall near the base of the bed said it was just after four. She'd heard them talking about a storm and the observatory. She wasn't ready to give up the blessed peace of Tim's touch just yet. Even as she told herself her desire to keep his heavy arm across her stomach was all about the painful electrical zingers that would start hitting her the second contact was broken, she knew it was a lie. A big, fat, hairy fairy tale.

Careful not to move a muscle, she studied him for the first time, unconcerned with being caught or questioned. He was solid muscle poured into soft denim jeans and an even softer t-shirt. Basic and elemental. He could be featured in an ad campaign for football, sports drinks, or a clothing company. Something about him screamed authentic, patriotic, strong. He reminded her of her brother, sharp mind and steel will determined to do the right thing. The rocking body was an added bonus.

She traced the outline of his features with her gaze, solid jaw, furrowed brow, straight nose and crow's feet at the corners of his eyes from a life of sun, stress, and taking care of other people.

And the scar. She couldn't see where it began, but it wrapped around the side of his neck and disappeared under the collar of his shirt. Her fingertips ached to touch it. She wanted to lay her palm over the Shen imbedded there and claim him, make sure he knew, unequivocally that he was hers. Forever.

The urge didn't make sense. It was totally, utterly, and completely illogical, but she didn't care. She didn't know him, not really. She knew the basics of his story, ex-military. She knew he was a pilot. She knew he had an adorable little dog who bossed him around and that he liked to fish. He blushed when she'd carried Bandit out of the shower wearing his clothes. He'd tried to salvage her hair from the lake fiasco. And he'd held her when she'd cried. She knew enough to want him.

Raising her arm from where it lay draped across his chest, she lifted her hand toward his cheek. The need to touch his bare skin exploded to life inside her like a bomb going off in her chest. It actually hurt.

The heat from his right cheek buzzed through her palm where it hovered a hair's breadth away from making full contact.

Four words echoed through her mind with a vicious and unrelenting fervor. His voice. 'Did you say mate?'

Pull yourself together, girl. He doesn't want a freak.

Everyone who knew her, who loved her, was gone. Dead. Her parents, her brother, her grandmother. No one left. That's why she'd been chosen. Taken. But it still stunk. She was alone in a crowd, again. Cue the music.

Regret made her arm feel ten pounds heavier as she dropped it back to her side and closed her eyes. Tears gathered beneath her eyelids, but she took a deep breath and told them to leave her the hell alone. She didn't have time for a breakdown. Pity party over. Time to put her big girl panties on and deal. Time to pull her championship fight out of its hiding place and bring out the mentally tough leader her teammates had relied upon time after time. She never gave up. Didn't matter if the score were fourteen to zip and the opposing team had the serve. She. Did. Not. Quit.

Sarah took a deep breath, gathering her willpower to move away from him and get up. Time to get moving and deal with the buzzing pain she knew would hit her as soon as she left his side. She couldn't lie here another second feeling sorry for herself and wanting what wasn't hers. She had to move...

"No." Tim's hand slid down her side and his fingers circled her wrist where it rested against her hip. "Not yet."

Sarah's eyes popped open and met his sober gaze.

"Shh. It's okay." Tim lifted her hand and pulled it slowly forward. He settled her hand on his cheek, rested it there a moment and moved her touch to the space behind his ear, to his scar. "It's okay."

She heard his words. The heat of his flesh melted her insides until she was a hot jumble of zinging nerves encased in skin. But her entire concentration focused with laser-like precision on his mouth, inches from her own.

His gaze held her frozen, waiting for some outward reaction to his movements, to his touch.

She had none to offer. Her entire reason for existing in that moment became to stare at his lips and imagine them pressed against her lips, her skin…everywhere.

Beneath her palm, his Shen pulsed and hers answered, shooting desire straight to her core. His hand covered hers, trapping it in place while his heart leapt to life in his chest. She could hear its frantic pounding as Tim gasped and arched his back off the bed like he'd been shot with a jolt of energy.

Ω
Chapter Five

She was aware of his gaze locked onto her face, of the bowstring tightness of his muscles. She knew of the pounding of her heart and the burning tingle at the base of her spine. But none of it mattered.

He twisted toward her, lowering his lips to cover hers in a nearly mindless rush. The world faded away and her body simply flowed toward him like an ocean tide rising to meet the sand. She parted her lips beneath his, accepting the kiss even though the rational part of her brain was screaming a warning. *His* name would be seared into her consciousness forever. There would never be another kiss to match this. No man would ever measure up in her mind against *this*.

He pulled her atop him until she was lying over him like a blanket, trapping him beneath her exploring mouth and hands. She wrapped her fingers around the sides of his head, locking him to her with a single-minded passion she'd never experienced before. He was suddenly her air, her heartbeat. Nothing existed but his soft lips moving against hers, the intensity of his invading tongue, and the feel of his strong hands gripping her hips so tightly she was claimed…completely.

Or was he simply unsure of what to do with his hands while she lay on top of him molesting his mouth?

He'd started this. He was kissing her back. His tongue invaded her mouth to duel and dance with hers, mimicking the act of making love until she was prepared to rip her clothes from her body and beg him to take her.

And perhaps he would. Evidence of his arousal pressed against the sweetest spot and she fought back a groan as she pulled her mouth away. What the hell was she doing? Any red-blooded male would get a hard-on with a woman draped all over them. She had discovered his 'automatic arousal button' by touching the mark on his neck. It was chemically and biologically programmed into him now. But that didn't mean he wanted *her*.

Just like that her brain started functioning again. Time to end the fantasy and get back to real life.

Unable to resist one more sweet moment of bliss, she rested her lips against the side of his neck and inhaled the electric scent of him. The hot spice of his skin surrounded her and she closed her eyes to savor it before facing the music. A few seconds became several minutes. Even as she damned her weakness where he was concerned, she couldn't pull away yet. She needed to absorb as much bliss as she could to take out and savor later, to give her strength when she stood facing the monsters who would destroy Chicago.

Everyone she loved was dead. Perhaps he could become her reason to fight.

"Are you all right?" Tim's hands stroked up and down her back in a slow, tortuous glide as his breathing slowed to normal. So gentle. So kind.

So not real. She'd thrown herself all over him, and now shuddered against him like a weakling child in need of reassurance. Saving Chicago was her duty. No one else could do it, no matter how much she wished otherwise. She had no doubt that mister military hero would volunteer if he could. But impossibilities didn't interest her right now. And that included fantasizing that this man could actually have feelings for her after a few hours.

Was she all right? Hell no. But she'd learned how to put on the public face a long, long time ago. And no matter how much she wished otherwise, he was still the public. "I'm okay."

"Hey in there! Wake up, sleepyheads! It's time to get moving." Luke's loud voice and quick double knock at the closed bedroom door threw off the last of her sensual haze and she jumped in shock, then quickly rolled to sit beside Tim on the bed.

"Thanks. Be there in a minute." Tim answered as he made a grab for her wrist before she could get up. He missed and she quickly moved across the room to where she saw her shoes at the base of an overstuffed reading chair.

Lowering herself into the plush seat, she reached for her shoes and wobbled for a moment as the buzzing pain hit her again. After several hours of rest, the shock and pressure of the energy flowing through her made her gasp.

Tim rose from the bed and moved toward her, but she put up a hand to stop him as the light bulb in the decorative lamp sitting on the bedside table exploded. Then the alarm clock on the opposite table went off.

"No. I got this." Sarah closed her eyes and shut the flow of energy down the way the Archiver had taught her. Focus through the pain. Control the flow. Send it where you want it to go.

Tim hovered like a mother hen, but she ignored him and

pulled the energy back to bearable levels. The alarm clock stopped and she put Tim's flip flops back on. The plastic helped stem the flow of energy as well. That was good to know. When she wanted to get crazy, she could stand on metal barefoot.

But not today. Today that would just make her head explode. The loss of more than one vital organ in one afternoon would be more than she could take. She was a fighter, not a liar. And since her parents' and her brother's deaths, she'd never lied to herself. No doubt her heart had officially surrendered to that earth-shattering kiss. The traitorous organ was no longer hers. But unless Tim suddenly decided to claim it, the poor little muscle would have to deal with the fact that they were down thirteen to one in the final game and didn't have the serve.

"I'm ready." She looked up at Tim to find him waiting at the door. He nodded and held open the door for her.

Time to get to work and figure out how to save millions of people in the real world. Time to get over delusions of romance. A kiss was just a kiss.

A hot kiss. An all-encompassing, body-burning, make her want to rip his clothes off right now kiss.

But she didn't get to do any of that. And she wasn't sure he wanted her to. He was a certified, grade-A, American hero. He'd do anything to save the lives of nine million people. And he'd play along with her if he had to. So, how was she supposed to know if he liked her, or if he was just doing his job? Did he find her attractive, or did the 'auto-on' switch on the side of his neck simply scramble his brains into a thoughtless, lust-filled mess?

There was no way to know until after. She couldn't put

her heart out there on a maybe and get it stomped on again. She had enough end-of-the-world doom and gloom on her plate without risking a broken heart. And didn't that just stink?

* * *

Tuesday, 7:45 PM

Sarah leaned back in the passenger seat of Alexa's sleek sedan. Alexa waved and accelerated. Tim let the girls pass by and take the lead on the highway. Alexa had insisted on some alone time with her fellow time-traveler, and Sarah had jumped at the chance to put more distance between them.

Tim rubbed his hand over his bald head and cursed himself six ways to Sunday. He'd been a damn fool moving on her like that. But God help him, he'd woken the moment her breathing changed and held himself still while her touch hovered and tempted. The force of his need for that simple caress on his face had shocked him and he'd stopped breathing, waiting for it, until he felt her emotional withdrawal. Her sad resignation and rejection of her own desires.

How he knew what she was feeling, he couldn't say. It had been odd but so instinctive, he hadn't questioned it. The flash of fire in his veins when she'd finally touched him drove all thought from his mind. In that moment, he hadn't questioned anything. She'd simply been his. Gorgeous. Smoking hot. Kissable. His.

Then she'd run like a scared rabbit.

Sarah's face had twisted in pain when the energy hit her. His damn head still buzzed like a hundred fat flies were divebombing his ears from the inside. He couldn't imagine what must be going on with her. But she'd distanced herself from him after scorching his insides with that kiss. Despite the fact that he'd probably regret it, if Luke hadn't knocked on the door, he knew he could have seduced her, buried himself inside her so deeply she'd never get him out.

But that was bat-shit crazy thinking. He had nothing to offer her but hot sex and his tactical skills on this mission. The longing he felt in her, the sadness, could only be healed by fairy tale bullshit, and he just didn't believe in fairy tales any more. People lied. People died. And he had nothing to offer a woman but a lifetime of looking over her shoulder and waiting for a sniper's bullet.

They'd figure it out. Eventually, when someone finally deciphered his equations and realized he'd corrupted them all, they'd come for him. Until they did, he had to pretend to be normal, innocent, and rock solid. Lies. Lies. Lies. No woman deserved that.

To add insult to injury, the most annoyingly happy human he'd ever met whistled non-stop from the passenger seat of his truck since they'd left the house. Twenty-seven minutes parked outside the mall while the girls shopped and now the drive to Hancock Observatory. Alexa had insisted that Sarah have some clothes that actually fit her. He liked her just fine wearing his. It was stupid and absurd to want to keep her in them when they had to go out in public and present the facade of normal, everyday tourists. But damn it all, that's what his irrational brain wanted. Evidently, he was now officially thinking with his dick.

Judging by the happy glint in Sarah's eyes when the girls had come out of the store, the wait had been worth it. She now looked sexy as hell in a pair of stretchy jeans, a rust colored, lace trimmed cami, and a cream colored hoodie. He'd preferred watching her walk around barefoot in his home, wearing his clothes and no underwear, but that was a dangerous train of thought. He did his level best to dismiss the memory of her soft heat draped over his chest. The pulse of her hand against his neck had sent a lightning bolt straight to his core like she'd flipped a damn switch. He'd locked his grip at her waist and hung on to his sanity by a thread. That woman was bottled lightning, in more ways than one. His death grip on her hip bones had been the one thing keeping him from rolling her beneath him on the bed and claiming her in the most elemental way possible.

So, yeah, getting her out of his clothes was probably the smartest thing they could do right now. The primitive brain that protested the move could shut the hell up. He had bigger problems, like figuring out how to stop an attack on American soil.

He shifted in his seat to take the pressure, and his mind off the growing problem there. Luke had the balls to laugh at him from the passenger seat.

"It's just going to get worse, you know." Luke crossed his arms over his chest and frowned at Tim like a disapproving father.

"What?"

"Everything."

"If you say so." If Luke was determined to give him a lecture, it was going to be a long drive.

"Look, Tim. I've been through this with Alexa. Only with her it wasn't just Chicago. If she'd failed, several billion people would've died, and it would've been my fault. I trusted the wrong people. Don't make the same mistakes."

Tim thought about his team, and about how his first thought had been to call them in. But he hadn't made the call.

They would've laughed at him if he'd told them everything. So, he would've had to lie to get their help. He couldn't ask them to risk their lives and not give them the truth. "Don't worry. I won't."

Tim drummed the fingers of his right hand against his thigh in time to the beat on the radio and hoped Luke was finished.

"Don't underestimate her, and don't leave her side for an instant."

"Got it." Who did this guy think he was talking to? He held his tongue out of respect for the women, but Luke was getting on his nerves worse now than when he'd been whistling.

"No. I don't think you do." Luke sighed and ran his hand through his hair as if the weight of the world were on his shoulders.

"Look, Luke. I appreciate the pep talk, but I've run more ops than you can imagine. I think I can handle this."

"No, you're being a fucking idiot."

Tim raised an eyebrow and didn't dare speak. He'd rip the guy a new asshole and lose a possible link in the chain. And Sarah'd never forgive him. Ten more minutes in this fucking truck, and he was done with science boy for good. He'd find another way to keep Sarah hidden on the observatory until after they closed for the night. Luke and his invisible wife could just go home and let him do his damn job in peace.

Luke shifted in his seat and Tim felt the other man's challenging glare focus on his face.

"She doesn't trust you."

The accusation stung, but it was true. She didn't. "She

will."

"If she doesn't trust you, she's as good as dead. You better fix it."

Tim shook his head in disgust. "I'm working on it."

"No, you're not. You're too busy trying to figure out how to use her to track that ship. Too busy trying to decide whether or not to believe all this, or if we're playing you for some kind of fool."

Tim had no response to the latter, so he focused on what he could respond to. "If this is for real, that ship will be responsible for millions of deaths."

"It's for real."

Okay. He'd bite. "What convinced you?"

"Alexa knew things no one could know. She could also disappear into thin air. And I dreamt about her for sixteen years before she showed up in my kitchen rummaging for food. I knew she was mine the moment I saw her."

"Sounds like a fairy tale." Tim had no one to blame but himself. He'd asked. He wouldn't make the mistake again. Luke obviously had…issues.

"You better start believing in fairy tales."

"I appreciate the information, Luke. But I don't have time for fairy tales. We've got a ship to find and a weapon to destroy in the next two days. And Sarah…" He trailed off, not sure what to reveal of his thoughts. If she could do a fraction of what she claimed, and control it?

Luke clenched his jaw in anger, like he was reading Tim's mind. "Sarah's not a weapon. She's not an asset you can deploy. She's a woman who will leave your ass behind if she thinks you are manipulating her, using her, or if you make her feel like she can't trust you."

"She's a volleyball player, for Christ's sake. Not a soldier. She's a beach bunny with no training who blows up light bulbs. How is she going to stop an alien ship with advanced weaponry? I haven't called this in because no one would believe me. But that doesn't mean I won't do everything in my power to stop it from happening."

Luke thumped his head against the headrest behind him in frustration."Hell. Alexa was right. It's even worse than I thought."

Tim ignored the outburst. The poor guy was losing it. *Civilians...*

Luke turned in his seat and leaned forward, right hand on the dash. "You are not listening, but I am going to tell you anyway. Listen to me or don't, it's up to you. But I've been through this. The Archiver doesn't make mistakes. He sends women who can do the job. Powerful women. Alexa's family has stories going back hundreds of years. The Timewalkers are not to be fucked with. This is serious. Nine million people in Chicago are going to die on Friday if the woman riding in that car doesn't trust you with her life. If she doesn't trust you, if she doesn't believe that you've got her back, if she isn't one hundred percent sure that you'd die to protect her, she'll leave you behind and try to tackle this thing alone. She'll die. And nine million innocent people will die with her while you watch.

"She's yours. It doesn't matter whether you wanted a woman in your life or not. This isn't a military op you can macho man your way through. You can't go kill something or blow it up. You have one job, keeping her alive. Beyond that, anything you might think you wanted became irrelevant the moment that mark burned into your neck."

Tim pulled into the parking garage and made sure his face was a cold, blank mask. "Look, I appreciate the help you've given us. But why don't you take Alexa home now and get out of town. I've got it from here."

"No, you don't." Luke and Tim both focused on the women as they climbed out of Alexa's car, deep in discussion. Alexa looked worried, and Sarah's eyes were as wide as a frightened rabbit about to bolt.

Luke pulled a flash drive from the front pocket of his brown slacks and handed it to Tim. "I made a call. One of my friends at the lab is working on geomagentics. High level, experimental stuff. Above Top Secret. I got some ideas from him on what the weapon could be and thoughts on how to reverse the magnetic charges. Stuff like that. I tried to get it into layman's terms, but some of it's physics theory, and there's just no way to get around it."

"Thanks." Tim carefully tucked the drive into his own pocket and looked Luke straight in the eye.

"I'm giving this to you because you're marked. I'm going to trust you to do the right thing when the time comes and not get my ass thrown in prison, or worse, for smuggling that out to you."

Luke was right. If the flash drive held what Luke said it did, the man had just placed his future and freedom in Tim's hands. Could be a set-up, another lure, but that didn't feel right. None of this felt right. "I'm doing my best, here, Luke. I don't know what you want me to say."

Luke put his hand on the door handle and paused. "Don't say anything. Just do whatever you have to do to get Sarah to trust you. Lie to her. Seduce her. Tell her you love her, even if you don't yet. I don't care what it takes. If she isn't convinced that you are madly in love with her, that you'd die for her, by Friday morning, game over. She's dead. You're dead. And Chicago is gone. I almost lost Alexa. I know what I'm talking about."

They got out of the truck and Tim locked it up as Sarah approached him with her head down and her arms wrapped around her waist in a defensive gesture. Pain transformed her face into a web of crow's feet wrapped around glassy eyes, but she didn't reach for him or the relief he knew his touch provided. Luke watched as well and raised his eyebrows at Tim to make his point.

Go ahead, rub salt in the wound.

Luke was right about one thing, she didn't trust him yet. And she certainly didn't love him. He doubted she ever would. He was too scarred, too hard, and too used to being alone. But he could convince her to trust him, seduce her and lie to her if he had to. Because the truth was, he *would* die to protect her.

Death meant little to him. He'd seen it too much to fear it. He risked his life protecting others. It's what he did. It's what every soldier did, every day. It was part of his fucking DNA. For eight years that had been his whole life.

Sarah was not going to get hurt, no matter who was involved or what he had to do.

Seduce. Deploy. Protect.

Should be a piece of cake.

"You guys ready?" Alexa wrapped her arm around Luke's waist and gazed up at her husband.

"Time to ride the lightning." Sarah's smile didn't reach her eyes, but she led the way to the elevators.

Ω
Chapter Six

Wednesday, 12:04 AM

They huddled together in a corner with Alexa munching non-stop on energy bars. Did the woman *never* stop eating? It was dark, the Chicago lights lay below them like a carpet of multicolored stars. The elevator ding alerted them to the final descent of the night. The lone security guard had wandered the observation deck and cleared it. Now he'd go home to his family and she'd get to work trying to track an alien spaceship.

Even thinking the thought was odd. How bizarre her life had become.

"Did you kill the security cameras?" Alexa whispered the question and Sarah answered.

"Yes. They're toast."

"Good. I was getting tired." Alexa released her hold on the light, or whatever it was she did, and suddenly Sarah could see everyone clearly again. Feeling Tim's long, lean form pressed against her spine in the dark had been a sensual distraction she didn't need. Alexa wasn't the only one desperate to get out of the corner.

Sarah dashed for one of the giant windows and looked out over the urban sprawl crawling with life and energy. In two days it would be gone forever unless she figured this out.

"Good luck. We're here, in case you need us." Alexa wrapped her arms around Sarah's waist and gave her a fierce and painfully tight squeeze. "Remember what I told you."

Tim's alert gaze flicked between them but Sarah refused to reveal the highly personal nature of their girl-talk.

"I will. Thank you for all your help."

Alexa let her go and walked to Tim and gave him a quick but brutal squeeze around his shoulders. "You ready?"

Tim nodded but Sarah saw the flash of doubt in his eyes. He still didn't believe her, at least not about everything. It hurt. "Ready as I'll ever be."

Sarah wanted to argue, but thought better of it. He didn't believe the ship was out there. It didn't matter. She knew and had asked Alexa to take Bandit with her when she left town tomorrow. At least she could keep the little beast out of harm's way. Bizarre as it was, knowing that even if she failed, that little ball of fluff would survive, brought her a small sense of peace.

Timewalkers had failed before. Many, many times.

"Good luck!" Alexa and Luke backed away to give them room, disappearing around a corner to a now abandoned hallway to wait for them, as planned.

She was now alone at the top of the world with the sexiest man alive.

Tim reached for her hand and frowned when she deftly dodged the contact.

"I can see the pain in your eyes, Sarah. Let me help you."

Shaking her head, Sarah moved until she stood inches from the glass. "No. I need all my energy to scan the skies for that ship. I'm not sure how this is going to work, and I don't want to hurt you."

That wasn't the complete truth, and judging by the raised eyebrows, clenched jaw and tight lips, Tim knew it. The truth was she couldn't bear the comfort of his touch right now. She had a big battle to win tonight in bending the energy to her will and searching for the alien ship. She didn't have the will to fight her heart, too. The traitorous organ yearned to be in his arms again instead of standing alone thousands of feet off the ground with the weight of millions of lives on her shoulders.

The big, epic adventure stories with heroes who faced impossible odds to save the world were fun to read.

Living this reality required an entirely different mindset. This was more than a game. This was a championship death match between her and the bad guys. If she could eliminate their best play before the opening serve, she'd win.

"Let's go to the top." Tim swept his arm like a true gentleman, waiting for her to precede him into the stairwell.

A few minutes of climbing and they emerged onto the roof of the building. It was cold now, with the thunderstorm coming in off the lake, and Sarah was glad she'd bought the warm hoodie. The sales clerk had laughed at her. It was June, hot and humid, but not up here. Up here it was bone-numbing cold. Sarah wasn't sure if it was the actual temperature affecting her, or her own fear stealing the warmth from her bones.

Nothing stops fear faster than action, lovebug. Granny T's voice whispered to her from memory.

"Okay, Tim, I'm going to send the energy out into the skies and try to find them. I don't know how to describe this to you, but I think it's like sonar. I think I'll be able to read the energy patterns in the air like bats use sound."

Tim nodded, but his intense gaze stripped her bare and exposed her terror. Thankfully, he didn't comment on what she knew must be in her eyes. "I'll keep watch."

Of course he would. She'd seen him catalog every exit, every stairwell, and every rooftop within sight of their position in the hour they'd spent wandering the deck as tourists before the building closed. No doubt he knew the layout of the streets below and three alternate exit plans were simultaneously floating around in his head. He never stopped watching, never stopped analyzing, and never stopped thinking of her as a tactical weapon.

Maybe, when this was over, he'd think of her as a woman. Assuming they survived. And what if they did, but she failed in her mission and Chicago burned? Could he live with that? Could she?

No. She couldn't. Standing there, with the lights and life of Chicago spread before her, the knowledge that she'd either save these people or die with them settled in deep, a cold and calculated mantle of conviction that melded to her skin and filled her bones with dread. She could not live if they all died. The babies, the kids, the cute grandma's with curly white hair and warm cookies in the kitchen.

She had to do this.

Sarah chose the north facing edge and stepped out as far as she could go before closing her eyes. She allowed the buzzing in her head to expand and grow.

The energy of movement, of friction, swirled around her like currents of noise in an ocean as the wind blew with its usual enthusiasm.

Mentally, she grabbed onto the energy of one of those wind waves and rode with it until her awareness was high above the tower. She latched onto another current and rode it even higher, repeating the process until she was no longer Sarah St. Pierre, but part and particle of the storm. She became simply wind and wild kinetic energy rippling over and around Chicago with as much riotous abandon as any ocean storm. She was a hurricane of magnetic current hopping to and fro, flitting from molecule to molecule as the gases and vapors in the sky danced around one another.

It was beautiful and enthralling, and Sarah wanted more. She willed the powers of the storm to answer her call, to coalesce and tease one another in a high-powered waltz between air, water, and the charged particles of dust and pollution which joined the dance, changed the molecules, fighting for supremacy in the mix.

Lightning struck a tree near the lake below and the bolt fired through her consciousness with the clarity of a completely formed thought. She *was* the lightning bolt. She *was* the joyous burst of light and fire that exploded into the tree and burst, exultant, into the ground.

The resulting crash of thunder shook her physical body, momentarily drawing her attention back to the sad limitations of the physical form standing with arms wide open, head thrown back staring into the storm with wild eyes that did not see.

That form was small, and weak, and Sarah had no desire to return to it. She turned away and glided on the currents in the sky once again, calling lightning in a rush of pleasure so intense it thrummed inside her essential self with each strike.

The storm grew and spread out over the lake until the waves crashed over the manmade barricades and onto the streets, all because she willed them to. The sweet thunder of the surf, the power of it relentlessly pounding the ground, added to the wild energy at her command until her awareness expanded beyond the pulsing of the city's electrical grid, the thunder and howling winds. And there, higher than she'd dared go before, nearly to the limits of mother Earth's atmosphere was a calm, cold, controlled ball of energy that would not respond to her. It rested like an anchor in the chaos straight above the city.

The ship. She'd found the ship.

The moment the thought formed lightning surrounded the ship in a cobweb illuminating strikes.

She'd kill them now and be done. She'd win this match and they could rot in hell.

There was no Chicago, no people, no Sarah of flesh and blood. There was only the wild call of the storm and the seductive pull of power. She called to the charged ions flowing through the highest levels of the atmosphere, speeding and clashing against one another at nearly light speed through the sky. Just a bit more and she'd order the energy to invade each individual particle on that ship. All would be vaporized in an instant.

If she'd been human, if she were still tied to flesh and bone, she would smile.

* * *

Tim grimaced as another gale of wind pushed at the limits of the building. He felt the concrete and metal sway under his feet in response to the storm's attempts to topple it. Lightning flashed repeatedly, illuminating the Chicago skyline like a giant sparkling strobe light. There was no break in the flashes of brilliant white fire, or the howling wind that beat against everything in its path with unrelenting force.

Sarah stood, immobile, head thrown back, arms splayed wide as if she meant to embrace the stars. He didn't dare move too close, but he knew her eyes were open and the electrical buzz surrounding her was causing visible sparks of electricity to fire off his clothes every time he moved.

He could deal with that. Hell, he'd been shot at, stabbed, nearly drowned, had his friends blown to bits next to him and held them bleeding to death in his arms. He'd faced just about every combat nightmare he could think of.

He'd never been this rattled.

He could handle piss-your-pants scared, but standing there helpless while a slender, doe-eyed female threw lightning bolts around like softballs? Sarah swayed and the skies raged in response. She sighed, and the lake surged over the barricades and pounded the streets. The wind had nearly lifted him off his feet more than once. The elements answered her call, just as she'd claimed. And to top it all off, she battled an unseen enemy without him. A cold-blooded, murderous, plague-inducing alien enemy from another time…

He growled and paced the side of the deck, keeping her in sight and scanning what little he could see of the surrounding sky for attack. Sarah was stirring up a shitload of chaos. If he were the commander of that enemy ship, he'd aim a missile at the top of this building and take her out with one shot. If he knew where she was. Hell, the bad guys might not even know she existed. Wasn't that the whole point of pulling her out of her own time? No one would miss her? She was alone and untraceable.

No. She wasn't alone. He was here. He was definitely here. And research or no research, Sarah was what she claimed to be. No one could stand next to her on this rooftop and doubt her incredible power.

Relief flooded him that at least one problem was solved. He could believe her now. No more doubts or second guessing. Thank God, because that kiss had taken his proverbial knees out from under him. There would forever after be two distinct phases of his life, two different realities in his head, pre-Sarah and post-Sarah. Pre-kiss and post-kiss. Now that he knew her touch, he'd never be able to forget the fire that coursed through his veins when she'd laid her hand over the mark on his neck. Pure lust had exploded through his bloodstream and the mark had throbbed with awareness of her every moment since.

Until now.

Tim frowned and rubbed at the scar on his neck, trying to awaken the mark again. Nothing. It was dead and silent, numb, just like it had been before Sarah had dropped into his life with all the subtlety of an earthquake.

Numb, as if she'd cut the invisible connection between them with a finely honed blade.

What the hell was she doing? How could he ground her, or keep her from blowing herself to pieces, if he couldn't feel the energy building inside her? How the hell was he supposed to keep her alive if she cut him off?

The strobe light effect of the storm's lightning strikes nearly blinded him as he took a step toward her.

In his right front pocket his cell phone vibed at him. Quick check of caller I.D.

Luke. Shit.

"Tucker."

"Stop her right now. She's attacking the Archiver's ship."

Tim didn't answer, just ended the call and slipped the

phone back in his pocket. The woman standing before him with her arms raised looked like a goddess come to life. The rain danced and the wind blew in a futile effort to reach her. She stood untouched in the eye of the storm. He was soaking wet, leaning into the wind, and half deaf from thunder.

"Sarah." Tim closed the distance between them until he stood inches away. She didn't respond. Not even a flicker of an eyelash.

"Sarah!" He raised his voice and stepped in front of her, squeezed himself into the two feet of space that magically separated her from fury around them.

Her sightless eyes were focused on something far from here and did not see him. She remained frozen in place and unmoving, like a mannequin. No spark in her eyes, no *life* in her face at all.

She looked like a standing corpse.

The phone in his pocket buzzed again. He ignored it.

"Sarah, come back to me. You're attacking the wrong ship." Tim braced himself for electrocution and placed his palm on her shoulder.

No response. Not even a sizzle.

He gently shook her.

Nothing. She was gone. What stood before him was a shell, nothing more.

"Damn it." Tim ignored the wrenching pain in his chest. He was losing her to the storm. He could feel it. The numbness of his mark spread down his back like a cold smear of jelly.

What would happen to her physical body if her mind, her consciousness, her very soul didn't return to it? A coma? Death?

Of course, she'd die, you dumb ass. And that smug bastard, Luke, warned you this was going to happen, warned you that the Timewalkers were something more, something so far beyond his experience that he hadn't been able to comprehend what she was capable of.

How the hell could he? If the wind and lightning weren't about to tear the top off of the building right now, he still wouldn't believe it.

A startling array of lightning snaked across the sky in a giant web of light unlike anything he'd ever seen before. It stretched for miles across the sky. A second later thunder literally shook the building he stood on. Car alarms sounded throughout the entire city in an eerie, collective scream from the ground.

He was a highly trained soldier, a killer when he had to be, but she could fry him with a twitch of her little finger. It was intimidating and humbling. This Archiver had chosen him to watch over her, to help her learn control. Failure was not an option. He couldn't let her fry the whole fucking city trying to take out the wrong ship.

"Sarah!" Tim grabbed both shoulders and shook her briefly, looking for a spark of recognition. Still nothing. The cold spread down his back, through his buttocks and into his legs. Weakness followed and he realized what he felt was her leaving him behind. He'd grown so used to the additional heat of the mark continually pulsing on his neck that the absence of its warmth was now a shock to his entire system. She was shutting off his internal sun and the cold darkness of night couldn't wait to take over and drown him from the inside out.

Lightning struck the corner of the building two floors

below them and sizzled through the wind and rain. The outer layer of glass beneath their feet cracked with a loud tinkling explosion of sound. Enough. She might be in control of this incredible storm, but he wasn't taking any chances.

Tim swept her off her feet and carried her into the building, off the roof and away from the call of storm and sky. She was limp as a rag doll in his arms as he raced down the stairwell to the heated main room they'd left behind just minutes ago. And she was cold. Too cold.

She was dying. As she drifted farther away from him and merged her energy with the storm, every beat of his heart was an echo inside a cold, dead cave.

He'd been promised more a few hours ago. Much more, and suddenly he wanted it all. True love and all that happy mumbo-jumbo, namby-pamby bullshit he made fun of his buddies for but never succumbed to himself.

So what if he had secrets, and enemies. She did, too. And hers were bigger and a hell of a lot scarier than a bunch of military brass in lab coats or behind sniper rifles. She needed him.

You're hers and she's yours. You better come to grips with that fast or you two won't survive. Luke and his big mouth.

Tim sank to the floor against a pillar and settled her across his lap, her beautiful cheek pressed to his chest, her sightless eyes staring straight through him.

His phone slid out of his pocket, but he let it go and lowered his lips to cover Sarah's in a gentle kiss. Their cold and unmoving softness angered him.

"Come on, Sarah! Snap out of it!" Determined to wake the Sleeping Beauty in his arms, he lowered his lips to hers and tried again. Still nothing.

His head ached with the possibilities of failure and he rested his forehead against hers and held his lips centimeters above the soft pink temptation of her mouth.

He wanted to kiss her lips, sear her body with heat and claim her. He moved his left arm up from where it rested across her waist to her shoulder, then gently slid his hand to the side of her neck where he covered the cold skin surrounding her Shen with his hot palm.

Instantly her heartbeat pulsed through the mark and her body shivered in his embrace, awakened to the cold numbness of being left behind.

"Come on, Sarah. Come back to me." Tim whispered the words against her lips and crushed her chest to his, trying to warm her up. They were inside a heated building, and she still felt cold as a corpse. "Come on, come on, come on."

The pulse beneath his palm grew stronger and his legs no longer felt like they'd been filled with cold jelly. But it wasn't enough. He wanted to burn. He needed to know she was fire and light to his darkness. He desperately wanted to feel again, and he realized he never could without her. It still didn't make one damn bit of sense but he no longer cared. She was his. He would not lose her like this.

Gently nudging her face with his nose, he stroked her cheek with his cheek, and nibbled and tugged gently on her lips in a constant assault.

The steady beat of her heart grew strong and he smiled as he felt its pulse reach all the way to the mark on his neck, flooding it with heat.

He buried his nose in the soft satin of her hair and nuzzled her ear. "That's right, Sarah, come back to me."

She gasped in the deep sigh of a woman who had nearly

drowned and arched in his arms as she awakened from death's sleep to whisper his name.

His internal temperature skyrocketed from cool and worried to flaming lust in three heartbeats and he claimed her next breath with a kiss meant to both punish her for nearly leaving him and demand submission to his claim on her.

She melted into him, wrapping her arms around his neck, and locking him to her with arms like steel chains around his back. She was sleek, muscular, and strong, and that flipped every damn one of his switches. He burned for her. There was no thought, no conscious decision to invade her mouth with his tongue. He simply had to be there, had to taste her, feel her skin beneath his palms and bury himself in her wet heat. It was not want or thought, his need took over like animal instinct and he knew he was more dangerous in that moment than he'd ever been on any mission or combat situation. If someone or something tried to hurt her or take her away from him in that moment they would die.

Even the thought made him crazy, mostly because he hadn't listened to Luke's warnings. This was his fault. He'd nearly lost her and he had no one to blame but himself.

Never again.

He kissed her with renewed vigor and moved his right hand down her back to the hem of her hoodie. Gliding his hand beneath it, his fingers swept up beneath the bottom seam of the soft cami and caressed the still cool skin in the curve of her lower back and side.

Her mark pulsed white hot beneath his left palm and she gasped his name between kisses, shaking in his arms.

Never in a million years would he have planned to get naked with a woman on the floor at the Observatory, especially not when it was their first time together. But he hadn't planned on her either.

A low rumbling noise penetrated the red haze of Tim's mind, but he ignored it. It came again, closer this time, but Tim pulled Sarah more tightly against him and continued to explore the hot depths of the kiss.

Something hard pelted him in the shoulder and he lifted his head, ready to kill anyone or anything that threatened.

A man's large brown shoe lay on the ground where it had fallen.

"Snap out of it, Tim." Luke waved his arms in front of his face like he was a rabid dog and he was afraid to be bitten. "We've got to get the hell out of here, right now."

Alexa's disembodied voice drifted to him from the elevator doors. "Hurry, Luke."

Tim's every instinct switched to operations mode as he registered the panicked sound of Alexa's voice and matched it to the coiled energy dancing behind Luke's eyes. Luke's easy-going, good guy persona hid a highly trained, Einstein smart threat.

"You're military, aren't you?" How the hell had he missed that?

"Not technically." Luke grabbed his shoe and bent down to lift Sarah from his arms.

"Don't." It was the only warning he was going to give. Tim stood and gingerly allowed Sarah's feet to hit the floor. They collapsed beneath her and she fainted. Tim scooped her back up. He hugged her tightly in an attempt to combat her body's severe shivering. "You a company man?"

"No." Luke walked to the elevator and stepped inside, blocking the open door. "You in here, baby?"

"Yes, I took care of the camera but we've got to go."

"I know." Luke wrapped his arms around air and held the door open as Tim stepped in with Sarah. Luke punched the button.

"So, who do you work for and what's going on? Do we have company?" Tim gritted his teeth as the doors slid closed, trapping them inside. He leaned his shoulder into the elevator wall to keep his balance as the steel beast lurched beneath their feet and began its descent. His mind warred with instincts as he continued to hold Sarah. He couldn't get to a weapon fast enough to defend them if he needed to and he couldn't bring himself to dump the shivering, semi-conscious Sarah on the ground either. The conundrum had his pulse pounding. The pressure in his chest built until he was sure one of those freakish aliens would erupt from his sternum at any moment.

"Once we reach the bottom you'll have to cover us all as we head straight out. We don't have time to sneak around." Luke leaned down to place a kiss on the now visible Alexa's forehead then turned to Tim. "The people I work for don't exist, and don't know these girls exist. They are irrelevant. We have to get the hell out of here because while Sarah was attacking the Archiver's ship, the real bad guys picked up Sarah's energy trail. The Archiver says we've got less than five minutes to get the hell out of here."

Ω
Chapter Seven

Tim studied Luke's protective stance and watched the man wrap his arm around his wife's waist with a worried frown and tense shoulders as they rode the elevator system down. Luke stood and moved like Tim did, like a hundred other guys he'd known and fought with over the years. The guy was combat trained, and more, if Tim didn't miss his guess. But Luke disarmed with a smile and friendly cheer. That screamed company man. He was a damn wolf in sheep's clothing to be sure. How the hell had he missed it?

He'd been too distracted by the flesh-and-blood woman in his arms to pay attention to all the details. That kind of mistake would get them killed. A science geek, a diplomat, and a killer all wrapped up in one perfectly charming package? Hell yeah, he could see where that could come in handy. Not necessarily *more* useful than an engineer who could trigger a trap and eliminate an enemy from miles away, but still useful.

"Sorry about the shoe, but I prefer to keep breathing."

Tim snorted. Like he would've killed the guy. Fuck. He might have, if Luke had been stupid enough to come up on him. He'd been completely out of his mind. Dangerous. And stupid. He couldn't afford those kinds of mistakes. "How are they coming in?"

"By air, in a cloaked ship." Alexa rubbed her temples in slow, delicate circles. "If Sarah could've held out longer, she could have brought them right to her and tried to take them out."

Which was, of course, his fault. Luke's grim expression and Alexa's tired, gray-tinged skin tone was worse than the most guilt-inducing lecture he'd ever received from his mother. His fault. He didn't do his job and ground her properly so she could keep her energy surges under control. He was the weak link on the team.

Before he could even attempt a response, the elevator dinged and Alexa placed her hand on his shoulder from behind him with Luke covering his wife's back. Luke wrapped his fingers gently around his tiny wife's upper arm and Alexa gave the orders now.

"Walk straight out to the street. Side door, right corner leads to a stairwell with a one-way exit door that'll get us out of here. I'll hold the light as long as I can."

Tim walked and tried not to notice that everywhere Sarah came into contact with his body felt like dry-ice pressed to his flesh. Her shivering had nearly stopped, but he wasn't sure that was a good thing. "Sarah's getting cold again. We've got to hurry." All he could think about was getting her into a tub of warm water. Naked.

Don't go there...

"Put her hand on your Shen. You dropped the connection when we started moving." Luke's suggestion sounded more like an order, but Tim didn't argue. He shifted until he could grab her left hand and lift it to the mark on his neck. Heat blossomed and spread down his neck, through his chest, and reignited the attention of the reckless and obsessed second brain in his pants. But Sarah sighed and snuggled closer instead of flopping like a limp ragdoll in his arms.

They made it to the street and moved as a synchronized marching unit for a block and a half. Thirty feet and they'd be under cover of the parking garage. The streets were empty and Tim cursed under his breath when Alexa's hand left his shoulder. Nothing like painting a big fat target on their backs with an alien spaceship hunting for them.

"I'm sorry. I can't..." Alexa didn't get a chance to finish before Luke scooped her up and jogged for the cover offered by ten stories of concrete and shadow.

"Shhh. It's okay. We're almost there."

Tim jogged beside him carrying Sarah until they hit the inside of the garage. He wanted to put Sarah down and search the skies for their enemies, he needed to know what they were facing, but he didn't dare. Maybe he could...

"Keep moving, Tim. They're out there, but you won't be able to see them." Luke shouldered past him and Alexa's face was briefly illuminated by one of the dim garage lights. She looked nearly as strung out as Sarah did.

"Are you okay?" Tim couldn't help but ask.

Alexa smiled wanly. "As long as there are snacks in the car, I'll be fine. I blew through my last protein bar half an hour ago and I've never hidden four people at once before."

"Don't worry, angel. I brought chocolate covered peanut butter bars." Luke opened the door to their car and settled Alexa in the passenger seat then reached onto the floorboard behind her and pulled out a small cooler. Alexa grinned and slid back the lid. A sigh of bliss and a quiet, "I love you," fell from her lips.

Luke kissed her and closed the door. Tim quickly

averted his gaze and walked to his truck. It wouldn't do to be caught watching that little interaction, especially when he wasn't sure what Luke might see in his eyes.

Luke followed and scowled as Sarah began shivering again the moment his touch left her.

"She's a mess."

"I can see that." Tim wanted to kick something. His field medic skills didn't apply to shocked-out super-human women who could shoot lightning. Give him a laceration or good old-fashioned bullet wound any day. At least he wouldn't have this helpless panic turning his stomach into a volcano.

"It's too dangerous for Alexa here, and I won't risk it." Luke held out his hand and Tim shook it.

"I agree. Get out of town." Tim nodded toward Alexa's car. "Where you headed?"

"South. We've got a friend a few hours from here. You've got my number. I'll do whatever I can from there, but I won't risk Lexa again. Especially after seeing the power Sarah threw around tonight. She can do this, if you help her figure it out. This one's all yours."

Tim nodded and they both walked to the driver side doors of their vehicles. Luke paused and closed his eyes, like he was listening to something no one else could hear. Tim watched him with interest. More secrets...

Luke opened his eyes and met Tim's knowing gaze without apology or explanation. "They're gone now. Get out of here, get her warmed up and take care of her."

"I will. Thanks."

"Good luck." Alexa blew him a kiss, both hope and resignation in her gaze as the car sped out of sight, out of town, and out of danger. He really wished they had the luxury of following them.

Tim started his truck's engine and turned the heat on full blast. Sarah was unconscious again, shivering. Her lips were purple and he could see the thin blue vessels in her too-pale eyelids like veins running through cold marble. As gently as he could, he repositioned her on her side and rested her left cheek against his thigh. His fingers trembled as he pulled the hair away from her neck to expose the mark there. A tangle of twisted emotion clogged his throat as he lowered his hand to the mark. Everything he'd seen and felt in the last few hours coalesced into a jumbled mess in his head.

Nothing made sense anymore, except Sarah.

Warmth spread through him again and he rested his head back, closing his eyes for a couple minutes to embrace the feeling. He wanted this. He wanted her. In less than twenty-four hours he'd gone from ignorant bliss to this all-consuming need for a woman.

Love at first sight? Lust? Alien interference? Fate? Some thousand year old man playing cupid from a spaceship? The answer didn't matter to him anymore. She needed him. She was brave, powerful, and sexy as hell. She also didn't have a clue how to protect herself.

He did. Now Luke's lecture made sense. He got it. Alexa and Sarah were both powerful. They were both frightening in what they could do, and what their powers could be used for. They needed serious protection.

And someone to trust.

Glancing at the innocent dusting of freckles on her cheeks, Tim knew she wasn't cut out to fight alone. She was soft and scared. She was a nuclear bomb inside an eggshell. So he'd be hard for her. He'd kill anything that looked at her funny, and make sure she didn't crack.

Of its own accord, his thumb traced the soft contours of her neck and jaw as warmth continued to pulse between them. Yes, he would take care of her now, whether she liked it or not. And if that meant he couldn't stop touching her, he wouldn't stop.

Good thing the truck was an automatic.

* * *

Wednesday, 8:34 AM

Sarah woke in a rose scented bubble bath. The hot water soaked into her aching body and relieved some of the pain in her limbs, but none of the agony inside her head. The hard plastic knots of the strap adjusters on her cami bit into the back of her shoulders. They were pressed into her skin by the hard wall of muscles she leaned against.

Tim. She was in a bathtub with Tim. "Where are we?"

"My house. Just relax. We almost lost you out there."

The Triscani had attacked her, sucked the warmth from her soul. Memory flooded her, and with it came a dose of ice cold panic. Cold, inhuman creatures. The Archiver told her they were nasty. That man had a serious talent for understatement. Her head jerked forward and physical agony sliced through her skull at the sudden movement.

"Shhh. Don't move. I've got you. You're safe now." The heavy weight of his forearm rested just beneath her breasts and her temple was pressed against his neck. His other hand wrapped around her neck, over her mark, tempting her with the pulsing heat of his heartbeat. He held her in place, wrapped around her like rope around an anchor.

He thought she was safe, protected by his strength and his arms. He had no idea just how wrong he was about that.

She'd have to leave him behind. There would be no other way to protect him from the hunters she knew were coming. The other Daviss, the Triscani horde. She'd seen them in the storm, too. But far better that they hunt her now than find their true prey. She'd bait them, then lead them on a wild goose chase across as many continents as she could manage. She needed time. The girl needed time.

She relaxed into his embrace and let the soft scents and Tim's touch soothe her battered mind. The bathroom was lovely, with white roses and ivy entwined in the designer tile lining the walls. Soft pink and lilac tones bathed the room in a woman's soft touch. The intricate lattice of roses and color kept her eyes occupied and her mind calm as she floated in the warm in-between, not quite fully alert. She felt like she was waking from a dream that just wouldn't let go. A nightmare, really, that she recently escaped and was in no hurry to return to.

But she didn't have much choice. She'd made sure of it. She'd dealt those bastards a blow they wouldn't soon forget. They'd hover over Chicago like a dense lake mist now, afraid to leave her here. They had to hunt her down; they needed to kill her even more than they needed to burn down Chicago. Because she knew the truth. She had discovered the answer to the Archiver's thousand year old question.

She knew what they were after, and she'd burn in hell for eternity, stay on the run for years if that's what it took, to make sure they didn't get it. They'd never find the girl now, not as long as Sarah lived.

The drain had been incredible, nearly killed her. She hadn't expected that. But when you have to literally hide someone's energy signature through time and space, it takes a lot out of you.

Now Sarah needed rest, and she needed to try to lure them away from Chicago. She'd lead those bastards on a merry chase all around the globe, go somewhere storms raged constantly so she could keep her protection around the child. The beautiful, perfect child.

Sarah didn't know the girl's identity, didn't want to. The more conscious minds focused on the child, the harder it would be to shield her presence from the eyes of the Archiver, the enemy, and time itself.

No one could know. And that included the well-intentioned man holding her so tenderly in the water.

There was no room for him in her new life. No room for Alexa, the Archiver, or any of the thousands who'd died to get her to this place in time. Today, in that storm, she'd met the future in the crystal clear twinkling of a child's mind, and no one could know the girl existed. As long as Sarah lived, the bastards out to destroy this world and another would never be able to find her. She needed to protect the girl, give her a few years to grow up and harness the power and knowledge within her. Once that was done, it would be too late.

Sarah closed her eyes and enjoyed the precious warmth of Tim at her back and the still warm water surrounding her. She reached down the long tendril of power that ran from her heart to the child's and pulled energy from the wind and electrical grid of the house, pushing it toward the girl in a swirl of chaotic design. She wove a net of power around the girl's heart and mind, a web meant to hide and disguise her from discovery. Judging by the way her previous work had begun to unravel and fray around the edges, she figured she'd bought the girl a few months, a year at most.

She'd need at least ten more to grow into some semblance

of a woman, to be big enough to fight these bastards on her own.

She reached for more power and Tim growled in her ear. "Stop it." He gently shook her shoulders and broke her concentration. Sarah allowed the energy to dissipate with a tired sigh.

"Sarah, stop messing around. Your temperature just dropped again and I felt you pulling energy. What are you doing? Trying to kill yourself?"

Sarah clenched her jaw to prevent it from chattering. She was cold again. Hell. It was going to be a long ten years. "Sorry."

"Tell me what's going on. Talk to me. What happened out there on that rooftop?"

Sarah shook her head and let the tears pool behind burning eyelids, then slide silently down her cheeks and into the water. She couldn't tell him. His conscious knowledge that the child existed might increase the drain on her energy, make it more difficult to hide the child from the world.

A man like Tim didn't deal in half-truths and lies. He wouldn't be able to accept it. She wished she had some way to tell him that wouldn't endanger him, the child, and herself. However, she seriously doubted he'd be willing to globe-trot with her, always on the run from aliens hunting her, and never know why.

The knowledge twisted in her gut like a dull serrated knife.

Sarah pulled out of Tim's grasp and tried to stand. The now tepid bath water glued her cami and underwear to her flesh and she shivered as goose bumps rose to cover her from head to toe. She'd swear even the fine hair in her eyebrows rose in protest of the chill.

"Stop." Tim grabbed her wrist and held her in place. Her flesh pulsed beneath his touch on her arm and through her foot as it bumped his bare leg beneath the water. He had boxers on, by the looks of them, and every square inch of exposed chest and strong legs made her want to weep in regret. He was magnificent, and now he could never be hers.

"I'm sorry, Tim. I can't answer any questions. I need to leave Chicago as soon as possible." He frowned, but didn't release her.

"Where are we going?"

"We? Tim, I can't tell you why I need to run and I'm not sure I'll ever be able to." Sarah watched the pain and denial flicker across his gaze, followed by steely determination. Oh, he'd agree now. But she could tell by the grim lines around his eyes and mouth that he would demand answers eventually, answers she could never give him. "I think it's better if I go alone."

She pulled her arm from his grasp and stepped out of the tub. She lifted her second foot out of the bath and broke the last physical contact she'd had with him.

A staggering weight hit her and forced her to the ground. God, did she suddenly weigh five hundred pounds? Her diaphragm worked valiantly to pull air into her lungs and she struggled to her hands and knees.

So, this was the weight of her burden. It settled in and she forced her mind to calm. She could do this. She'd just have to pull a bit more power and use some of it to push the energy around her into a sort of cocoon, a shield of sorts, instead of a lead weight that crushed her like five G's of gravity pulling on every cell of her exhausted body.

"This is bullshit, Sarah." Tim crouched beside her but didn't touch her. "You need me. You can't even stand up right now. And I bet your temp is dropping, too."

Sarah looked into his calculating gaze and didn't bother to deny it. The uncontrollable shivering had already begun twitching its way across her shoulders and back.

Tim gave her mercy and placed his hand on her shoulder. Immediately she could breathe again, and the shivering slowed to random quivers between her shoulder blades.

"You can't do this without me, Sarah. And I won't let you try." He pulled her to stand facing him, both of them dripping onto the plush pink rug beneath their feet. "Just tell me where we need to go. What do we need to do?"

Sarah bit back sobs of relief. She'd tried to keep him safe. Was it her fault the stubborn man wouldn't leave her to it? "They'll hunt you, too, if you're with me, if you're protecting me."

Tim's entire body tensed at the threat. "Who, Sarah? What's going on?"

"I don't think the evil beings who were going to burn Chicago will care about that any longer. Their only goal now will be to hunt me down and kill me as quickly as possible."

"Why?"

"I can't tell you that without jeopardizing everything."

Tim studied her face for long moments. His gaze penetrated to her very soul, but she refused to look away. "Coming with me is as good as signing your own death certificate, Tim."

Understanding dawned and a pain-filled grin flitted across his features, then was gone. "You trying to protect me, sunshine?"

She felt the telltale blush creeping up her neck and knew her face would be bright pink in seconds. "They *will* hunt me. They won't stop until I'm dead."

Tim pulled her against his chest in a tight embrace and she went willingly, starving for the heat of his body and the false sense of security he wrapped around her like a baby blanket. "We'll see about that. We'll just see about that."

They stood like that for several tense seconds before Tim pulled back and lifted his hands to each side of her face. "I'm hard to find and even harder to kill." His thumb skimmed her lower lip in a featherweight caress and she stopped breathing, caught in the fire of desire in his eyes, paralyzed by the want bubbling through her veins. "I'm a predator, Sarah, not prey."

"They'll kill you to get to me." Sarah whispered the fact and rubbed her cheek into his warm palm like a cat craving his touch. "I don't want them to kill you."

The admission cost her what little pride she had left. She was pathetic. Too weak to walk away and protect him, and too needy to deny his touch. Tim ignored the threat to his life as if it were of no consequence and continued to tease her lower lip with his thumb. Anger flared to life up and down her spine. "Are you even listening to me?"

"Yes." Tim's lips dropped to hover so close she felt him breathe the word against her lips. "Every word. First they kill you. Then they burn Chicago."

Sarah shook her head and closed her eyes, waiting for the kiss she so desperately wanted. "It's not just Chicago." Her shoulders slumped. This wasn't right. She'd ask for nothing else from him, she'd done enough damage to his life already. As much as she wanted to rely on his strength, this was her job, her mission. She was the one who had been Taken, chosen…sacrificed for the cause.

When the Archiver marked Tim, he hadn't known about the child. Celestina didn't know about the girl, either. No one else knew that the girl existed. And Tim certainly didn't need to know that Sarah would be required to sacrifice her own life to protect the girl.

Sarah knew, and she refused to beg him to die with her.

"Then what do they want from you, Sarah? Why do you believe they will hunt you?" Tim kissed her cheek and she swayed in his arms, unable to stop the instinctive reaction to his nearness, his touch.

"Because I didn't leave them with any other choice. They have to kill me, or they'll never find her." The man had seduced the truth from her with a soft kiss at the corner of her mouth.

"Find who?"

Sarah opened her eyes. The sudden influx of light threatened to send her to her knees with pain. "I don't know who she is."

"Sarah." His firm grip stabilized her as he spoke against her ear, his lips skimming the sensitive flesh with every word. "We go together. I will help you. And, I will kill anything that comes after you."

She wanted to believe him, wanted to believe that he could…

"But you're going to have to trust me. You have to tell me everything."

"You don't know what you're up against. They're not human." Sarah pulled back and looked into his eyes, studied the strong, lean lines of his face.

Yes, he was undoubtedly one of the toughest men she'd

ever met, but tough didn't beat supernatural. The nasties hunting her wouldn't play fair, and they wouldn't play by human rules.

Ω
Chapter Eight

"I figured that one out for myself." Tim's fingers slid from her shoulder to her hand and entwined with hers, gently tugging her toward the towels. "Let's get dried off, then you can start talking."

Sarah nodded, rethinking her strategy. So she'd tell him what she knew. The burden she carried would buckle her without his help. She hated herself for being weak, for wanting to believe he could keep her safe, for putting his life in danger. But she couldn't refuse. Saving Chicago was one thing. She could throw lightning bolts and blast a ship out of the sky. Even dying in the process didn't scare her, if that's what it took.

But it wasn't about Chicago anymore. It was so much more. For some reason, the Triscani wanted this girl so badly they'd traveled through time to kill her. That alone was enough reason to make sure the child lived. Sarah was deathly afraid that she wouldn't be enough to protect the girl alone. Not enough. It seemed to be a lifelong theme. "Okay."

Tim pressed one foot over the top of hers before letting go of her hand to reach for a towel. He spread his arms wide, holding the giant white towel like a blanket and closed his eyes. "Wet clothes off."

Sarah didn't say anything, just stripped out of her wet

cami and let it hit the tile floor with a sloppy thunk. The undies stuck to her legs and she had to peel them down her body to pool at her feet. One foot she lifted free with no problem. The other was trapped under the firm press of Tim's where his arch crossed her toes. Her wet underwear lay over his foot like a cold, limp fish.

Sexy. Oh, yes. She was sexy. Who wouldn't want her and all of the save-the-world responsibilities that she brought to the table? As if the normal amount of emotional baggage weren't enough. She couldn't even stand up without him there to help ground her power, and her head still felt like an entire jackhammer crew was hard at work. God, she was a mess.

Eyes still closed, Tim stepped forward and wrapped the towel around her, making her feel like a giant burrito. She warmed the moment the soft cotton wrapped her up. Warmed because she was out of the wet clothes, or because he stood close enough to burn?

Tim turned as far as he could without losing contact and disposed of the rest of his clothes before she could gasp a protest. She should close her eyes, she really should, but the tight stretch of muscle across his shoulders and buttocks held her transfixed. She should look away, turn...something.

Blocked. White cotton fuzz interrupted her perusal and broke her lust induced trance before he wrapped it around his waist, blocking her view of his perfect, *perfect* backside.

"Shall we?" Tim held out his hand, and she tugged her own towel until it held tight across her chest before placing her hand in his. Once his fingers were twined with hers he lifted his foot and kicked away both of their underwear. The wet fabric hit the side of the bathtub and slid down to a combined puddle on the floor. Sarah stared at it, transfixed by the sight of something so intimate. She wasn't a virgin, but she'd never shared personal space like this and she didn't trust it, didn't quite believe he wouldn't run when things got bad. Scratch that. They were bad now, but they were going to get worse. Much, much worse.

She glanced up from their clothing to find him studying her intently. Waiting. *Shall we?* "Yes."

Ten minutes later she sat next to him, perfectly content in another of his oversized t-shirts and a pair of sweatpants. Her new clothes were still in the back of Tim's truck, but she didn't mind. These were dry, they were warm, and they smelled like him.

Pretty sure her cheeks were still flushed from watching him get dressed, she curled up on the couch in front of the dormant fireplace. She had hot cocoa in one hand and a peanut butter and jelly sandwich in the other. No gourmet meal in any hotel in the world had ever tasted better. Her bare feet were tucked securely beneath his denim clad thigh and she obsessed over the press of hard muscle she wiggled her toes against. Licking her lips, she couldn't tear her gaze from the tight stretch of white cotton over his chest and shoulders. The naked heat of his neck and head mesmerized her and she clenched the cocoa mug to curtail any unscripted movement.

Look with your eyes, not with your hands. Granny T's stern reprimand filled her head but didn't calm her libido.

She shoved her feet farther beneath his thigh and wiggled her toes again. She knew she baited a tiger, but she just couldn't resist.

Headache now a dull roar, thanks to some ibuprofen, the

pain killer allowed her to think. Thinking sucked. The enormity of her situation forced her to hold back the occasional attack of hysterical laughter. He already thought she was crazy. Why not confirm his suspicions by completely losing it?

Now there was a perfect plan.

"Stop that." Tim shifted and lightly swatted her calf. "You're getting a bit close to the boys."

That froze her wiggling feet in place but didn't bottle the grin she felt spread across her cheeks.

"How are you feeling? Any better?" Tim studied her like a doctor would a patient. Assessing. Critical.

"Yes. My head still aches a bit, but other than that, I'm fine." *Liar, liar, pants on fire…*

"Okay. I need to ask you some questions and I need you to tell me the truth. If I don't know everything, I can't make intelligent decisions about what to do."

Spoken like a true soldier. But then, what else did she expect? "All right."

"So, these aliens will try to track you down? How? How do they find you?"

A bitter laugh burst from her. "I don't know. They will try to unravel me first. When they give up on that, they'll try to find me in the physical plane."

"Unravel you? Explain." His intense frown left no doubt in her mind that he didn't appreciate her choice of words.

"I wove a web to protect me from direct assault in the energy field. I made sure it was big enough that it would be nearly impossible to find me in the tangle."

"And if they do find you?"

"I'm dead. Bolt of electricity to the heart. Easy kill." She took a sip of her hot cocoa and leaned back against the armrest of the plush suede coach she'd occupied just over twenty-four hours ago. A lot could change in a day...

Tim's eyes rounded in alarm and Sarah waved off his concern. "They can't find me that way. Trust me. I made sure of that."

He tilted his head and raised his eyebrows like she was a fool for believing her own words. Perhaps she was. "You're sure? They can't attack you with just energy?"

"Yes. Once they realize they can't break my energy shield, they'll decide a bullet in the brain would take care of the problem just as well and start looking for me in the flesh." God, was that calm, detached voice really coming from her? Wow. She was better than she thought.

"No. They won't." Someone wasn't calm about the idea. So much coiled anger vibrated through the words her head throbbed again in response.

"Yes, they will. If they can't kill me from afar, they'll try to kill me on the ground." She looked him straight in the eye, but he didn't budge. Not even a muscle twitched. She polished off the last bite of her sandwich and used her blessedly free hand to try to rub the pain out of her temple.

Tim watched her vain attempts to rid herself of the pain, then promptly reached across and pulled her into his lap.

"What?"

"Hush." Tim put his palm on her neck, over her mark, and soothing warmth flooded her limbs. He lifted her hand to the mark on his neck and held it there. The flood of heat was heady and the room spun around her as if she were drunk. She closed her eyes and pressed her now pain free head into his shoulder. No pain. Floating and spinning, but no pain. Just heat…

Tim's voice rumbled through his chest beneath her ear, and he sounded a bit out of breath. "So, how do they track you?" Tim's question tied her stomach in knots.

"I don't know. I just felt their intention. They've been here a long time. They know human ways." Sarah placed her free hand on his shoulder and mustered every ounce of courage she had. She *could* do this alone if it meant saving Tim. She would find a way to keep him out of danger. It would be hard, but a small, cold, and extremely calm part of her soul whispered to her that it wouldn't last for long. It whispered the truth to her with icy resolve. Deep within, where the energy built and gathered, she knew what it would take to buy the girl enough time to grow up. She was just having a bit of a hard time accepting how little time she had left.

Suddenly, she was fiercely glad that Tim wasn't in love with her. She was meant to be alone. She had a purpose. Tim would help her, could keep her alive and ease her burden long enough to get the job done. Then he'd be free. No pain. Everything was as it should be.

"Can you feel their approach? Will you know when they are closing in on our position?"

"Yes, I think so." It wasn't much, but it was something.

"Where are they now?"

Sarah opened her mind to the energy swirling around them and followed the threads she'd woven around herself outward until she reached the wide open expanse of this world, this time. Everything moved in a giant slosh of waves, energies dancing and crashing against each other like rolling tides and currents in the ocean. She knew what she was looking for, knew what their energy tasted like to her soul. It took her mere moments to find them, lightly probe the edges of their corrupted, evil natures, then retreat to her body, still warm and snug in Tim's arms. "They're still hovering over Chicago."

She opened her eyes to find Tim's gaze locked onto her face like a laser. First her eyes, then her cheekbones. His gaze roamed her features, then stopped and held on her lips.

"Maybe we should hunt them instead. Can you find their ship?"

"Yes. I think I can."

"And you'll feel them if they break through now? You'll have warning?"

"Yes."

"Thank God." He whispered his thanks and crushed her to his chest, his lips covered hers, demanding a response.

She was helpless against the onslaught of sensation. His masculine scent teased her nose beneath the subtle aroma of rose bubble bath. The reminder of the way he took care of her, held her, filled her head and heart with lust stronger than anything she'd ever felt in her life. He was perfect. Strong. Sexy. Stubborn as hell.

His hands rounded the curves of her waist and back. He shifted, laying her down on the couch and covering her. His hot body pressed her down into the soft leather at her back, lips never losing contact as his tongue sought entry into her mouth to taste her and explore. To seduce.

She wrapped her arms around his head and pulled him closer, her tongue dueling with his, tasting him as she ran her hands over his head and shoulders, absorbing the feel of him, the absolute power he held in such tight control. For the first time in her life she felt small, feminine, and beautiful. Desired.

The sensation was both heady and painful. All that coiled strength. All his intelligence and honor. He was perfect, the perfect man. And he wanted her. *Her.* There was no room for deceit in the power of his kiss, no hesitation in the firm touch of his hands as they roamed her body, no doubt of the desire that pressed so firmly against her through the fabric of soft cotton pants. Nothing mattered but surrendering to his touch. She didn't need to breathe, to think, to cry. She needed to feel, to give him everything.

At least once before she died, she was going to give herself totally and completely to a man. He couldn't love her, he couldn't know. But she would take him with her, carry this moment inside her soul and draw on its power. When she had nothing left, the memory of his touch, his kiss, would give her the strength to do what needed to be done. With Tim at her side, perhaps she could become a predator, too.

The moment he placed Sarah's hand over the mark on his neck he was lost. His entire body pulsed in time to her heartbeat and his need for her roared back to life with the fury of a beast twice denied.

So, he asked her what he needed to know. They had a few hours. Chicago was no longer the prime target. They wanted Sarah...

Over his dead body.

He kissed her because he had to, rolled her beneath his larger frame on the couch because he needed her to know she was his now, his to touch, his to protect, and his to claim.

The fact that she wore *his* sweatpants and t-shirt and they were caressing her naked flesh, were all that separated her from his touch, added to the animalistic knowledge that she belonged to him now. The couch he'd settled her naked body on just hours ago was large, plush, soft, and more than long enough to accommodate their six foot frames.

The chaos of the day swirled through his mind once again as he tasted her kiss. The image of her cold, non-responsive form at the top of the observatory fueled his need to explore her skin, to keep her hot, pliant, and soft as melted butter everywhere his fingertips roamed.

He'd had lovers. He'd started seducing the pretty girls in high school. Once he'd joined the military keeping a woman became too hard. Too many secrets he couldn't tell her, too many lies. His last girlfriend had survived eight months of not knowing where he was or if he'd come home. That was that. He figured it wasn't right to ask any female to put up with the demands of his life.

He'd been playing in the sandbox like an innocent five-year-old while people like Sarah, Timewalkers, were on the real front lines battling planet-wide destruction.

An invisible time-traveling guru had chosen him, Timothy Daniel Tucker, with his shaved head, burn scars, and tattoos to protect Sarah, to help her save the world. To love her.

Sarah didn't have a team of trained soldiers at her beck and call. She had no back up, no training, no group of knuckle-headed, rude, sex-starved, testosterone driven wild men willing to take a bullet for her. She risked everything for a nameless, faceless humanity.

The pressure would break most men he knew.

But Sarah didn't break, she arched her back beneath him and wrapped her arms around his head, locking him in place like a band of molten metal. Her hands roamed his head, feeling her way around the lumps and scars on his neck, clinging to him and his hard-ass head like she cared, like the rigid lines and uneven landscape there turned her on. Like she loved him.

No. He couldn't allow his mind to go there, to imagine her lips lingering on his old wounds and healing him from the inside out. It hurt too much.

He pulled away and lifted her t-shirt over her head, bared her to his hungry eyes. "You're beautiful, Sarah."

She didn't answer, just lifted her hips off the couch so he could pull the loose sweatpants down her legs and throw them on the floor. He wanted to taste the slim lines of her throat, the lean muscled legs and small, pert breasts. Every inch of her slender form was long, lithe and calling out to him to explore.

He shucked his own clothing in a frantic series of impatience and covered her, skin to skin. He reclaimed her mouth in a kiss meant to sear her to the soul. She'd never forget she was his. She'd never question again.

The two lamps at the ends of the couch flickered. Tim tore his lips away from her mouth so he could taste the column of Sarah's neck, her ear. His lips grazed behind her ear to kiss the mark there.

A jolt of power flowed from her skin to his lips and into his mouth before flooding his body with the drumbeat of her erratic pulse. The sensation traveled straight to his groin and he swelled to painful fullness.

She moaned his name and her legs wrapped around the

back of his as she opened for him and he settled against her core.

"You're mine, Sarah." Tim nipped at the sensitive flesh one more time and enjoyed the rolling flow of energy that buzzed through his bloodstream. "And I'm yours."

He stopped thinking then and let his body take over, go where it wanted to go, taste where it wanted to taste. His lips wandered down over her shoulder to tease her nipple. His ears filled with the soft sounds of her surrender as he continued to nibble and pull her soft flesh into his mouth. He shifted enough to allow his hand to slide over her petal soft skin, headed south, to her welcoming heat. He stroked her there until she panted his name, begging for release. Only then did he make the small shift and slide into the wet heat of her body, joining them at last.

Sarah cried out and arched her hips. She drove up against him until he was completely consumed by her flesh. He would have survived the exquisite pain of denying his own release if she hadn't chosen that moment to wrap her hands around his head, placing her palm over the sacred mark on his neck.

He stopped breathing. Air stopped moving, trapped in his lungs by the surging tide of electricity that swamped them both. The charge built between them. Everywhere they touched power flowed skin to skin, surrounding them in a bath of sensual energy. The heat built, concentrated where they were joined together. Sarah's fingers dug into him as the sensation tore him away from reality.

She whimpered as orgasm after orgasm rippled through her entire body. The wet heat surrounding him gripped his body, squeezed and massaged him with relentless fury.

The once flickering light bulbs popped and returned the room to semi-darkness. He didn't care. He wanted her to blow up the whole damn house from wanting him. He wanted to burn his touch into her soul and he'd sacrifice the building's wiring if that meant she'd be his forever.

He didn't have much to offer her. He was broken and scarred, ugly and hard. But he could protect her. He could kill for her. And he could give her this...

Sarah's mouth sought his and he complied, wanting to taste her sighs of pleasure. She found his hand with her own and guided it to the mark on her neck. He followed her lead, touched her mark and completed the circuit he somehow knew would change everything.

Pleasure rocked through them again and she sobbed his name as the next climax thundered through her.

He held on as long as he could, a marathon of erotic torture forcing him closer and closer to the edge.

He succumbed at last and bit back a shout as his own orgasm started in his toes and swamped his bloodstream like a blowtorch of pleasure wiping out all doubt, all fear, all thought.

When he could move, he nuzzled her neck with his nose and allowed the sweet scent of roses and sunshine sooth his soul. Sarah was his now. He'd kill anyone who tried to hurt her.

They lay entwined and he knew she felt it too, the ebb and flow of warmth, the pulses of soothing heat that filled his body with peace.

He rolled to the side and pulled her to lay across his chest before covering them both with the blanket. She wasn't ready to hunt for the ship just yet. He'd make her rest, then eat.

Then they'd figure their next move out together.

She fell asleep almost immediately. He had a long time to lay there, hold her, and think...

* * *

Sarah blushed as she pulled a comb through her still wet hair. Their lovemaking had blown her mind, her body, and her heart wide open to the soldier sitting across from her. They'd fallen asleep for a couple of hours, naked, limbs entwined, still connected in the most intimate way possible. It had been embarrassing to wake up and feel him still inside her...for about half a minute. Then desire had come roaring back as he shifted against her and his erection returned with a vengeance, filling her from the inside out. The sensation of him growing within her had triggered an immediate answering heat and they hadn't even tried to deny each other.

Sarah sighed at the memory. Tim was big. He was smart. He was brutal, unforgiving, and trained to kill.

Maybe he was perfect for her after all.

A quick shower, always touching, and now dressing in some more of her new clothing made her feel almost normal. Almost.

The hungry animal she saw lurking behind his gaze as he watched her shower then dress made her feel decidedly not-normal. Men did not look at her like that. They just didn't. Until Tim. She didn't even lie to herself about it. She relished his lust, reveled in the memory of their mind-blowing orgasm-fest. In fact, she wanted him again. She could still feel the firm surety of his fingers on her flesh, his mouth on her breasts, his lips and tongue tasting her like he could never get enough.

Jesus, that kind of attention could be addictive. She

flinched at the blasphemous thought. "Sorry, Gran."

Her grandmother would have washed her mouth out with soap for that one.

"What?" Tim sat across from her at the small table, bare foot covering hers beneath the chair, a map of Chicago on the surface with circles and grids.

"Nothing. Sorry."

Tim wanted to plan, to figure out the best way to hunt the bad guys' ship. He'd asked her the one question she hadn't thought of...what if the girl was in Chicago? What if that's why the bad guys were here? She couldn't leave. She had to defend the city at all costs.

They'd already spent a couple of hours poring over Luke's flash drive and all the data on geomagnetics and quantum physics. Theories and formulas and a bunch of words that may as well have been Greek. Tim was in his element. She was no help at all.

She wasn't stupid. She had a journalism degree and had planned to go to work in the field after she'd finished playing volleyball. But twenty-five years of life and discovery had passed her by. Newspapers were, according to Tim, dead or dying. Everything now was on the computer, out there in space somewhere in "the cloud" on his iPad gadget.

She tried to comprehend the changes, but found she didn't care right now. She needed to worry about survival before she worried about the future of journalism. That meant physics. Mathematical theory. She could understand general terms and ideas, but she wasn't a physicist or electrical engineer. Magnetics and electricity were beyond her ability to decipher and absorb in a couple of hours.

Especially when her mind was constantly preoccupied

with thoughts of getting Tim naked again.

Her attention glued to the steel-like strength of his shoulders and her gaze wandered the curves of his neck, jaw, and head. Her lips longed to follow.

Seriously, this was ridiculous. She wasn't a sex-starved teenager. She had to find a way to take out that ship before it could wipe out Chicago, and as much as the thought disappointed her, sex with Tim wasn't going to help her with that. She didn't know who the girl was. She only knew the girl's soul was young, and probably in Chicago somewhere. There were way too many people at risk to try to find her in time, nine million too many.

Ω
Chapter Nine

Maybe if she had ten years, Luke's telepathy, and no enemies hot on her trail she could find the girl. Even then, she doubted it would be possible. The child was powerful, but she was young and didn't have a clue why she was hunted. Sarah was still in shock trying to digest the fact that these enemies were dedicating so much energy into killing one little human girl.

Why didn't really matter. It didn't have to make sense. Maybe she should tell the Archiver and Celestina. They had power. Perhaps they could help her protect the girl. At the very least, they would be thrilled to have the first real clue about why the Triscani had come here, why they'd killed millions of humans and disrupted the timelines. A thousand years of battle and they'd finally have a lead to work on, a hint as to why the enemy had come back in time to Earth in the first place.

Poor girl was stuck with Sarah as champion. So, now she knew, it wasn't just Chicago these aliens were after, it was some innocent kid out running on a playground or learning her ABC's in school. But why? And how was she supposed to keep this girl alive when she had no idea who she was or how to find her? But whatever the reason, the Triscani and the Archiver had been at each other's throats for almost a thousand years. Must be save-the-world important. Then again, what wasn't with that grumpy, white-robed immortal?

No pressure, Sarah. No pressure at all. She'd felt like a cheater when she'd learned that Alexa's mission had saved six billion people and hers was just Chicago, a measly nine million.

Oh, wait. Oops. Make that nine million people to save and a thousand year old mystery to solve.

Way to one-up that tiny little blond. If she had a champagne glass she'd salute her horrible victory right now.

If Chicago were attacked, would the girl would go down with it? Was that why they were attacking a single geographical point this time? It was their best guess. Celestina did say the Triscani had never done that before...

This felt like a messed up version of 'Terminator.' She'd watched the movie a few months before the lightning strike that took her away from her old life. So, she was Kyle Reese, sent through time to save a kid, the aliens were the Terminator, and little John Connor was a girl.

Trouble was, Kyle Reese died in that movie. He won, but he died.

Did that make Tim her very own Sarah Connor? She studied the chiseled lines of his face and bit back a laugh. Her name was Sarah, not his. And the thought of him in one of the popular mullet-style 1980's hairdos didn't fly. She kinda liked his bald head and hard edges. She was stubborn and strong-willed, but she wasn't used to death and war. Battle. He was. She could see it in the ghosts behind his eyes and the alert way he moved. His vigilance allowed her to relax a bit and trust that he'd know if something went wrong. She could relax and think...about sex.

Crap.

"Okay, let's hit the northern edge and work our way south."

Sarah followed his fingers as his hand flowed from grid to grid on the map. "Okay."

"And you're sure you can take out the ship without killing yourself?" Tim's intense brown eyes focused on her face like laser beams, making it impossible for her to lie.

"I think so."

"You think so." Tim sighed and rubbed his head with a free hand, a frown on his face. "You think so. That's not good enough."

Sarah shrugged and sat up straighter in her chair. "It's all I've got."

"I know, sunshine. I know." Tim rose from his seat and her foot lost contact with his as he walked around the table to stand behind her. The energy overload didn't hit her like a sledgehammer this time, instead it stretched and pulled between them like invisible strands of warm taffy. She instinctively knew if he went more than a couple of feet away from her, those strands would break. But for now, it was enough to know she wouldn't be dropped to her knees every time her skin lost contact with his.

He felt it too, and smiled as his hands came to rest on the back of her neck and shoulders. He massaged the knots out of her tense muscles with pinpoint and painful precision. She let her head fall back against his stomach and relaxed into his care.

"We'll start up north. And this time you won't ride the lightning alone."

She nodded and closed her eyes, afraid he'd see the tears

that gathered despite her brain's fierce demands to stay strong. She would do what she had to do. She'd fight to the death if she had to. But she wasn't strong enough to resist the solace of his touch and found that she was no longer sure she even wanted to try.

***

Wednesday, 8:04 PM

They drove for two hours, her hand wrapped in the warmth of his between them in his truck. They fought traffic and hit the northern edge of Chicago along the shores of Lake Michigan as the sun was setting. Twilight. Perfect flurry of kinetic energy, wind shifts, and power flowing through the water as the top layers of the lake released the sun's heat back into the approaching night. A dense cover of clouds hovered over them from the high humidity and lingering warmth.

"Why did we start up north?" Sarah was curious. He'd been adamant from the moment they'd pulled out the map.

"A hunch." He shrugged and pulled into a parking spot, cutting the truck's engine.

"A hunch." Sarah raised her eyebrows and waited. There was more to it than that. She could feel it.

Tim stared out the windshield as he spoke. "I've always had strong instincts. I don't know how to describe what I feel. I just know sometimes. It saved my team too many times to count. It got to the point where the CO would lay out a mission and ask me if my gut was talking or not. Most times, I got nothing. Sometimes, I'd tell him to pull the plug or rethink it. I can't explain it. I would know where snipers were before they fired, or where a bomb was buried. Stuff like that. The guys started calling me Prophet, but our CO told them to stop. He knew how accurate I was. He knew the top brass would turn me into a lab rat or bury me in some company think tank and never let me out. In fact, I knew if I didn't quit I'd disappear."

"You're clairvoyant?"

Tim shook his head and finally looked her in the eyes. "Sometimes."

Sarah squeezed his hand in hers. She had to know. "What are you getting right now about this? About us?"

Tim's jaw clenched and unclenched several times before he answered her. "Not a damn thing."

"Well that stinks."

Tim burst out laughing and it completely transformed his face. She grinned back at him. "Yes. Yes, it does."

They got out of the truck and walked toward the shoreline hand-in-hand like a couple of goo-goo eyed teenagers. She couldn't resist the urge to swing their joined hands as they walked.

"So, you said after the last mission. What happened?"

Tim snugged the backpack strap over his opposite shoulder and lifted their joined hands to his lips to drop a quick kiss on her fingers.

"I said too much and the recordings got back to the wrong people."

"The wrong people?"

"Someone passed the tape up the line. I had to warn a couple of my team about a trap. I couldn't let them die. I knew I was being watched. The CO had warned me and the rest of the guys to tone it down and cover our asses, but it was either speak up or let them die."

Sarah brought his hand to her lips this time, and tried to

soothe him with a kiss. "So, what happened after that?"

They reached the edge of the water and Tim slung the pack off his shoulder and pulled out a blanket. After whipping it into place along the beach he sat with his legs out and made room for her to sit between them. "One of the guys on my team got a call from someone at Fort Bragg. No names. Top level secret hocus-pocus crap. They were asking a lot of questions about past missions, reviewing audio. I knew if they had access to me it would only be a matter of time."

Sarah settled between his legs and leaned back into the heat of his chest. "So, what did you do? You can't just quit, can you?"

"No. You can't." He pulled another blanket from the bag and spread it over her legs. His voice sank, full of bitter pain, and she immediately thought of his scar.

"Your injury wasn't an accident, was it?"

"No." Tim didn't try to deny it. "I had to take out the lab, destroy some equipment, and make it look like an accident. The burn was severe, but I knew as soon as I made the decision that I would survive it."

Sarah considered for a minute in silence as the waves crashed to shore in a constant steady rumble. "And what better way to prove you weren't able to predict the future than to get hurt?"

"Something like that." Tim wrapped his arms around her waist and pulled her snugly against him, her back to his front. Her mark hummed in blissful warmth at its proximity to his just a few inches behind her.

On impulse, she tilted her head back on her neck and twisted around to kiss him on the cheek.

Tim turned and kissed her full on the mouth until she

melted into a puddle of want right there on the beach. Took about ten seconds, by her generous estimation. Probably closer to five seconds, but who was counting anyway?

Tim saved her from embarrassing herself by breaking the kiss and resting his forehead against hers. Their breath mingled in the wind and strands of her hair whipped around to tickle them both in the face.

"You ready to do this?"

"Yes." She wasn't ready. She wanted to sit on this beach with Tim and pretend they were a normal couple in love, cuddling and watching the city lights to the south flicker on and reflect off the water. Romance, ambiance, simplicity. But that wasn't true and never could be, so why delay? She had Tim's arms around her. That would have to be enough.

Closing her eyes, she relaxed in his arms and let her mind go quiet, waiting for the buzz of information to start as she tapped into the energies around her.

All she could feel was Tim, his strong arm wrapped around her waist and the heat of his chest at her back. Even the flow of air molecules as he breathed in and out beside her. Fascination held her still as she watched cold particles flow into his body and heated, dancing molecules flow out. The world around her took on a new dimension, a hypnotic beauty. The waves crashed, ribbons of wind whipped and spun around one another in a million never-ending duels, and the fading light of the sun skittered around like sparkling golden pixie dust blessing everything it touched with renewed energy and life. She felt like she'd left Earth completely and entered a magical, glittering wonderland.

Sarah let her mind, her spirit float up out of her body and noticed a strange light hugged her body where it remained on the sand. The soft amber glow stretched between her body and Tim's, cocooning them and connecting them in a way she couldn't comprehend.

Before her heart could jump to conclusions or her body could distract her with all out lust, she let go of the beach and floated up into the wind currents like she'd done before, riding them like a falcon, using them to hunt.

She soared upward until she hovered about a mile above the northern edge of the city and waited, filtering energies as they passed through her, hoping to get another odd ping in her consciousness that would alert her to the enemy ship or to the child's bright soul. But all she felt was the frantic activity of humanity and their machines bustling around like busy bees, humming in a strange artificial rhythm at odds with the synchronicity and harmonies of nature's energies.

No wonder the world was mad.

Another presence bumped against that thought, a consciousness other than her own pulsed and flowed around her.

A woman. Not as controlled as Sarah, not as big in the world. Sarah could feel the stranger's mind struggle to maintain her place in the currents of existence that continuously ebbed and flowed in a great ocean of energy around them.

Sarah could squash her like a bug, rip the stranger's energy pattern into unrecognizable shreds to be absorbed by the rest of the worlds frantic systems.

Who are you? The soft, curious question fluttered to her, like a thought with butterfly wings alighting on her shoulder.

Sarah froze, debating. The Archiver hadn't told her about anyone else like her. It could be the enemy, could be a trap.

Or it could be a very unique young lady wondering who she was, thrilled that she was no longer alone in the skies.

Hello? Are you there? Can you hear me? The woman's voice was a bit stronger this time, perhaps closer. Sarah debated for a heartbeat more then answered.

I am Sarah. Who are you?

I am Katherine. I want to meet you. Where are you?

Sarah laughed in her mind, the wind currents rippled and spun around her like dancing fairies. *I am here, just like you.*

Here. Present. Touching the world with her mind and watching it swirl in a kaleidoscope of motion and life. Sarah was confused. Why would the woman ask or care where she *was* when they were both so omnipresent at the moment over both the city and the lake? Over hundreds of miles of airspace?

And no alien space-ship in sight. Damn it anyway. Had she really thought it would be that easy? The Triscani must have found a way to tangle their energies with the world's as well. She'd never be able to find them this way if that were the case.

Where are you, Sarah? I'm in Chicago...

The trailing question brought Sarah up short. This woman was in Chicago? The city to be charred in just over twenty-four hours time? Oh, and by the way, she just happened to have skills similar to Sarah's, to a Timewalker's? Something didn't add up. Katherine might be what she said she was, a woman out riding the wind, but the coincidence would have to be astronomical. The statistical likelihood of that was basically zero. So, that left the other option.

Anger fueled her as she brought the vastness of her being

back from the edges, pulled it in from miles in every direction and trapped the woman inside like water in a balloon.

Katherine panicked and Sarah wished she could grin, wished she found humor in the ugly task she'd set herself.

Katherine's reach was small, much smaller than her own, and Sarah felt like she was disciplining a small child once she felt the full weight of the other woman's mind and abilities.

Katherine fled back down the only unbroken energy path Sarah had left her, a thread through which to escape back to her own body.

Sarah followed the woman back to the passenger seat of a large van and waited, her energy subtle and small, flitting around the air molecules inside the vehicle, as she watched the woman regain consciousness and catch her breath.

Katherine had a gun strapped to her side and five men with her, coiled to strike.

"Holy God, she's strong." Katherine's voice filled the small space and the men tensed around her. "She's here. Close. Head north, she's on the shore. We can be there in a few minutes."

The man beside her started the van's engine. "You can track her?"

"I think so."

"Dangerous?"

The woman rolled her eyes. "Of course. But I don't think she's been trained. She felt..." there was a pregnant pause as Katherine struggled to come up with the right word. "She felt normal. I don't think she's foreign or military trained."

"All right. We'll talk first and shoot second. Let's go get her."

Sarah meant to follow them, to listen and find out who they were and what they wanted, but a soft touch of discord reached her senses and she knew the enemy searched for her. Perhaps she could find them first in the complex web of energies flowing above the city. They were hiding, as she was. It was the ultimate game of cat and mouse. And she had to win.

The strange woman and her van full of human soldiers would have to wait.

* * *

Tim held Sarah steady with one arm around her waist and pulled his pack closer with the other. He unzipped it and made sure his gun, knife, and cell phone were all within easy reach as he scanned the beach, the sky, and the ground around them continuously.

Sarah's body was like a live wire in his arms, buzzing against his senses with a constant flow of energy. Good news was his back and arms weren't tired, the energy seemed to feed straight into his body so he wouldn't tire, no matter how long he sat there. The bad news was he couldn't let go of Sarah to move around. They were sitting ducks and his instincts were screaming at him to get the hell out of there.

Hell of a time for his dormant alarm system to kick back on.

"Sarah." He spoke against her ear, hoping she would hear him, but knew it was futile. She was after something. He'd felt her attention shift, narrow, and focus on it a couple minutes ago. He wished like hell he was telepathic or something so he'd know what was going on with her. But no, all he got was this vague sense of dread and tightening in his gut.

"Sarah, come back to me. We need to get out of here."

The hair on the back of his neck rose and goose-flesh broke out on his arms. Final warning. He could sense a van moving toward them from the south. Someone was coming for her.

As quickly as he could he scooted out from behind her and settled her on her back on the blanket. He took one of her hands and did his best to wrap her fingers around his ankle as he crouched beside her. He scanned the shoreline for a place to hide but knew it was futile. Whoever was coming at them was tracking Sarah by energy, not by sight. Hiding behind a bush would be like hiding a steak from a dog and counting on him not to smell it.

Nowhere to hide. Maybe he could carry her to the truck and outrun them.

What he needed was for little miss lightning bolt to wake up and zap their van into next week.

"Sarah, come on. I need you back here." Tim shook her shoulder and felt a faint stirring in his mind, but she quickly left him with the sense that she was doing something important and couldn't come back right now.

It was like getting a psychic answering machine...*Please leave a message and I'll get back to you when I can...*

No matter. He didn't want to have to fire his weapon on the unknown people coming their way, but he would if he had to. Blow a couple tires and he could outrun them, at least for now.

That thought in mind he swung his pack over his shoulder and, gun in hand, scooped Sarah up off the ground to run for the truck.

Too late.

A chopper approached from the southeast, heading straight for them.

"Sarah!"

Again all he got from her was a 'not now' vibe. "Shit."

The loud roar of the helicopter got closer and the wind from the blades tugged at his clothing, sent Sarah's hair into a soft sway where it dangled from her unconscious form. He couldn't outrun or out-drive a chopper, and he wasn't willing to kill a fellow soldier without cause.

So, good news was the chopper was U.S. Military. Bad news was, when he looked down he saw the horrible light of a laser sight hovering on her chest.

Tim froze and shook his head as the screeching wheels of the van reached his ears, followed by the sounds of doors and several people moving in on his position.

A woman came into view first. Nearly as tall as Sarah, she had dark brown hair and eyes. She was slim, elegant, dressed like an uptight corporate executive in a navy business suit and white shirt. She held both hands up to assure him she posed no threat, frowned and waved off the helicopter.

To his surprise the laser sight vanished and the chopper backed off far enough for them to have a conversation without shouting.

The woman yelled across the twenty yards separating them. "Please put the gun down, sir. We just want to talk to you."

Yeah, right. He'd heard that one before.

Tim glanced over his shoulder at the chopper and the sniper patiently watching him through his scope. The woman and whoever else she'd brought along were between him and the truck and Sarah was, for all intents and purposes, comatose.

He didn't really have any options. The sniper on his ass and the woman in his arms made sure of that.

"Throw down your weapon, sir."

Tim opened his fingers and allowed the pistol to fall to the ground at his feet.

The woman took a step toward him and signaled behind her. Three men walked into view, all armed to the teeth.

Tim hugged Sarah closer and leaned in close to her ear. "Don't come back yet. Stay gone until we know what we're dealing with here."

He didn't know if she heard him or not, but she didn't move or open her eyes.

"Timothy Daniel Tucker. The Prophet. Why am I not surprised to find you here?" The man who spoke pulled his hat and mic from his head to reveal a face Tim had hoped never to see again.

"Rear Admiral, sir." Tim glared at the man he and his team had simply referred to as "The Weasel" and waited. His involvement eased Tim's worry over being killed, but roused the primitive animal inside him. The man was a liar and master manipulator. He was also freakishly intelligent and so high up the food chain everyone knew The Weasel answered directly to Sec-Nav.

Shit. Maybe they knew about Chicago after all. "Why are you here, sir?"

"That's a question for you, Tucker. What are you and this lovely lady doing out here?" The Rear Admiral glanced at the tall brunette beside him and she gave the barest hint of a nod before zeroing her gaze in on the still unconscious woman in his arms.

"Just enjoying the sunset. My date had a bit too much to drink. We were headed home when you arrived"

"We can help you out with that. Why don't you and your...date come with us. We have a few questions for you." The Weasel swept his arm back toward the waiting van and Tim calculated the odds of making a run for it. His muscles hummed with energy, like he could run with Sarah in his arms forever and not feel a twinge of exhaustion or pain.

But there was the chopper, the sniper, the brunette's intense gaze, and the two men fanned out from their position to block any attempts at making a theatrical exit. This wasn't the movies, and if those two brutes shot at him, they wouldn't miss.

"All right, sir. Let's go." Tim walked slowly, carrying Sarah toward the waiting vehicle and climbed inside with her head nestled against his neck. He hoped like hell she'd stay gone for a while. He wouldn't tell them anything. Hell, maybe he could gather some Intel of his own. If they got nasty, he could take it. It would be hell, but he'd been drugged, beaten, and put through it before. Sarah was a different story.

If they hurt Sarah, he'd find a way to kill every single one of the fuckers.

The woman slid into the passenger seat and the two goons sat one on his right and one behind him with a pistol pointed at the base of his skull in case he decided to get cute. Goon number one slid the door closed and Tim sat back in silence. It appeared the Rear Admiral didn't want to talk to him in front of his men, so he had some time to figure out how the hell they'd found Sarah.

As if in answer to the unspoken question the brunette's

eyes shifted back over her shoulder to study Sarah's face and he saw a flash of recognition in the woman's too serious eyes. She glanced to his face, then quickly away. Whatever she'd seen had surprised her, but she didn't say a word as The Weasel drove them to God knows where.

    Had she actually recognized Sarah? Shit. This wasn't good at all.

Ω
Chapter Ten

Sarah hovered over the beach, energy coiled and ready to strike should anyone make a move to hurt Tim. She could take out the helicopter in a heartbeat if she needed to, but she hesitated to kill these guys. They were obviously U.S. government and Tim addressed the man talking as Rear Admiral and appeared to know him personally. Best not to kill innocent people, especially soldiers like Tim who were, hopefully, the good guys.

Tim warned her not to come back into her body yet. She toyed with the idea of zapping them all unconscious with a jolt of electrical current to the brain, but she was about blowing ships out of the sky, not small, controlled surgical strikes. She'd have to practice in case this kind of situation ever came up again, but she wasn't willing to lobotomize these people for wanting to talk to them. Maybe they'd have some information. And she wanted to talk to Katherine, find out how she'd been surfing the skies with her. So she waited, and listened as they talked Tim into the van.

He carried her cradled against his chest with tenderness, shifting to make sure her limbs weren't hanging at uncomfortable angles and her face was protected from the scrutiny of the strangers confronting him. He couldn't know she watched his every move and could feel his determination to protect her. He was fierce and fearless. And he was hers.

She loosened the lockdown she'd had on her emotions and admitted to herself that she loved him. He might not love her back, might never love her back, but that became irrelevant. *She* loved *him*. She'd melt the brain of anyone who laid a finger on him, practice or no practice.

Freed by the thought, her spirit laughed and she watched Tim stiffen and shake his head as if he heard her and disagreed with her assessment of the situation.

Sarah zeroed in on the energy pulsing from his mark and used it to trickle a thought into his head and a tingling caress to his cock. *Don't worry, baby. If they touch you, I'll melt their brains.*

He smiled, shifted in his seat and dropped a kiss on the top of her head. She wished she could feel it, and his arms as they tightened around her, but the grin on his face was enough.

Joy flooded her as she realized she wasn't alone any more. Never again. He was hers, and she'd lie, cheat, steal, or kill to protect him. If these people thought they were going to prevent her from accomplishing her mission, they were in for a big surprise. She had a little over twenty-four hours until the attack on Chicago. She had time to find out more about these people, and Katherine's particular talent.

They got caught in traffic caused by an accident and spent several hours heading east out of the city. They drove into an underground parking garage at Fermilab to Tim's whispered, "Why am I not surprised?"

Sarah's soul buzzed with the masses of energy coming from the collider. Oh, yes, she'd have to be careful now. That kind of power would allow her to vaporize Lake Michigan with a snap of her fingers. What the hell were they thinking, playing God with that kind of energy?

Tim stoically carried her to a windowless room with a large metal desk and four plain, armless chairs that looked like they belonged at a high school assembly. One was behind the desk, two in front of it, and one against the bare white wall a few inches from the door. She guessed that's where the guy with the gun would sit.

Fat lot of good a gun would do them if they touched her man.

They shoved Tim inside and locked the door, left them alone for a couple of hours while they sat in front of their computer monitors like vultures, hoping she'd wake up, hoping she and Tim would be stupid enough to talk in the room and give them more information. What idiots.

Finally, the jerks gave up and headed down the hallway. The Rear Admiral was joined by two well-armed soldiers with really big guns. He opened the door and waltzed into the room with Tim like a king entering a dungeon. He really thought he was in charge. Tim stood between her body and the invaders, protecting her, and again she considered frying the creep's brain into mush.

Cold blooded murder didn't appeal. Darn it, anyway.

"Sit, Tim." The Rear Admiral indicated the chair next to the one her unconscious body slumped in, but Tim didn't move.

"Get comfortable. Please. I just want to talk to you and the girl. I've got some questions and we're all on the same team, here. Aren't we?" The Rear Admiral returned to the hallway, door open but leaving goon number one behind. "I'll bring you some coffee while my guys check you for weapons. Then we'll sit down and have a civilized conversation. All right?"

The door closed and locked the three of them inside.

"I've got to check you for weapons, sir."

"You've got my pack. Knife and gun were in it. I'm not armed." Tim's voice was devoid of emotion.

"I've still got to pat you down, sir."

"Fine."

"I need to check her as well. I need you to step away, sir." There was no apology in the man's voice, just a statement of fact.

"Not going to happen." Tim shook his head and waited for the man to make his decision.

"I'm sorry, those are my orders."

Tim put his arms loosely at his sides and waited like a coiled cobra, kept his leg just barely pressed to hers. "You will not touch her."

The big man eyed Tim's stance and the tone of his voice. "I don't want to fight you, sir. I'm just following orders."

"Then tell the fucking Rear Admiral I said I'd kill you if you touched her. How's that for an order?"

The big man grinned and backed to the door, amusement, not fear in his eyes. "May I quote you on that, Captain?"

"Absolutely."

The door buzzed and the grinning fool opened and closed it behind him followed by the electronic lock that buzzed and clicked into place. Two cameras were placed on the walls with a clear view of the room from both directions. Small fry. Sarah zapped them until their chords were smoking inside the walls and no more energy flowed along the wires connecting them to the spies sitting in front of their computer monitors. She overloaded the monitors and their hard drives next, enjoying the loud pop as their surge protectors blew and the insides of their machines melted. With a decisive bolt of energy, she took control of the lock on the closed door so no one could interrupt them. Satisfied, she settled back into her body.

Her eyelids felt heavy, but she forced them open and tipped her head back to take in the strong jaw and stubborn profile of the man standing over her like a guard.

"Hi."

Tim met her gaze and the heat she saw there nearly robbed her of breath. "Hi." He bent over and planted a too brief kiss on her lips. "Don't say anything, we're in a holding room and there are cameras and mics recording everything we do or say."

"I fried them." She stood up and wrapped her arms around him in a fierce hug.

"You did?" His arms came around her immediately, as if he hated the separation as much as she did.

"Yep." She snuggled her face into his neck, and inhaled the scent of his skin, ran her hands along the back of his neck and up over his bare head, over the intense ridges and angles of his scar and the sensual heat of the mark buried within it. "Locked the door, too. They can't get in and they can't see or hear us."

She kissed his jaw and his hands tightened where they gripped her around the waist. "Did you really threaten to melt their brains, or was that my imagination?"

"If they hurt you, I'll fry them." She whispered the vow

against his lips then kissed him again, full on the mouth, and put every ounce of her devotion into the contact. She couldn't say the words, but she could feel her love for him growing with every touch, every word...every kiss.

His arms wrapped around her, pulled her flush against the length of his body chest to chest, hip to hip, thigh to thigh, squeezing until she could barely breathe as he took control of the kiss and invaded her mouth, challenging her tongue to an erotic duel she had no interest in winning.

He broke the kiss and she resisted the urge to force his lips back to hers. He was right. This was not the time or place to do everything she wanted to his hard male body.

"Christ, woman. You're going to kill me."

A grin escaped, and she knew she must look like the Cheshire cat. She felt beautiful, sexy, and truly wanted for the first time in her life. The feeling was going to her head...and other parts of her anatomy. "No, I'm going to get us out of here."

"We need to tell the Rear Admiral something he'll believe, or they won't stop looking for us until we do."

Sarah frowned and relaxed in Tim's arms. "I don't care about your Admiral. I want to talk to Katherine. She was riding the storm with me."

Tim's eyes widened in surprise. "Do you think the Archiver sent her here to help you?"

"No." Sarah thought about the small touch of power Katherine used to track her. "I don't think she's one of us. She's not strong enough to help me during the attack. But I need to know where she came from and why she has any power at all. Maybe she's a descendant. The Archiver will want to know if there are others like her."

Tim nodded. "Okay. So, we find Katherine and talk to her, then get the hell out of here. We'll worry about the rest later."

Sarah ran a hand up and down his arm, gentling the tiger she felt lurking below the surface. Tim didn't like to be caged. "I can open the door anytime we're ready. Your stuff is on a table in the room next door."

"Let's go." Tim stepped away and entwined the fingers of their hands, tugging her toward the door.

"Not yet. Katherine's coming and I want to talk to her."

Tim froze. "How do you know she's coming?"

"I summoned her right after I locked the Admiral and his men in their computer room. Coffee? Right. They've been watching you non-stop since they dropped us in here."

The door buzzed and Katherine stepped into the room carrying Tim's black duffel bag, a grim expression on her face.

"Sarah. I can't believe you're actually here. She said you'd show up eventually."

Tim stepped between them, but Sarah moved to his side and placed her free hand on his shoulder to assure him they were safe. Katherine looked familiar, memories tugged at the edge of her consciousness and she studied the lines of the woman's face closely. "Katie-bug?"

Katherine nodded.

"Last time I saw you, you were four years old."

Tim looked between the two of them and relaxed his stance a fraction. "You two know each other?"

"She's my cousin's daughter." Sarah took a step forward. "How did you end up working with these people, Katie? That Admiral is bad news."

Katherine tossed Tim's bag at his feet and he knelt to check it. He leaned his shoulder against her thigh as he checked the clip and loaded his pistol.

"You won't need that." Katherine sighed. "I'm going to have to lie through my teeth to cover up this one."

"How did you end up working with these guys?" Sarah's curiosity wouldn't allow her to leave. Here was a member of her family, a piece of her past come back to life and she was shocked at the importance this woman suddenly had in her heart. Little Katie...

"There are a handful of us in the C.P. We have certain gifts..."

Tim snorted and stood, swinging his bag over his shoulder. "C.P.?"

"Casper Project. I don't have time to explain. It's a private research arm utilized by the military."

"Gifts, huh? I'm sure the Rear Admiral uses these 'gifts' to his advantage." Tim sounded bitter.

"Of course. Just as you used your gift to help save the men in your unit."

Tim said nothing, but Sarah felt the truth of the statement.

Katie continued. "I've listened to the mission records, Tim. Your foresight saved your men more than once."

"You're the reason the Rear Admiral started poking his nose around my team."

She shrugged. "Sorry, I didn't know you were with Sarah." She stepped forward and wiggled a set of car keys. "Let's go see what Grandmother Tilly left you."

Sarah's hands started to shake. "Granny T?"

Katie nodded just as a loud bang reverberated through the floor. "They've got the sledgehammer out. They'll be through the doors soon. Let's get the hell out of here." She gave Sarah a quick hug then rushed into the hallway. "The car's parked on level three, section B. No one will stop us. I've disabled the alarms and communications you missed."

Tim studied Katie's face but didn't move. "You sure you want to come with us? The Rear Admiral won't forgive or forget."

She smiled. "Yes, I'm sure. I officially left the premises over an hour ago. He'll blame it all on the mysterious woman you have with you. They don't have a clue who she is, and Sarah's prints didn't have any matches in the database."

Sarah studied the woman she remembered as a young girl with pigtails and skinned knees riding her tricycle with total abandon. "Thank you, Katie-bug."

"You're welcome." Katie led the way down the long, sterile hallway and they followed. "How many days have you been here?"

Sarah checked her new orange watch. Four in the morning. Sunrise was in a little over an hour. It was Thursday. Already. "Two."

"Tomorrow then?" Katherine's question caught her off guard.

"Yes. Tomorrow morning."

"Something in Chicago?"

"All of Chicago."

Katie nodded and picked up the pace. "I'll give you my cell, for after. We have a lot of catching up to do and I have questions."

Katie broke away and tilted her head at an odd angle

until they all heard the pop of a blown camera around the corner. "We'll head left until the hallway dead ends. Then take a right, past two doors then take the stairs down to parking level B3."

"Let's go." Tim grabbed her hand and tugged her along a barren hallway. It looked like an abandoned building, all white walls and stark lighting. No nameplates or numbers on any of the doors.

"The Admiral won't stop looking for you, Sarah. Especially after this spectacular get-away. You'll have to talk to him eventually."

Sarah shrugged. "Not until it's done." She jogged next to Tim as they raced down the hallway. She couldn't help the glance over her shoulder at her cousin, her family.

Katie kept pace behind them as if she hadn't a care in the world. Sarah let it go for now. There would be time to figure out what Katie was really doing with these men, or rather, what these men were doing with her. She obviously shared some small piece of Sarah's gift with energy, but nothing that could compare to the abilities Sarah possessed.

Was it genetic, then? Had the Archiver Taken her because she already had the gift and his meddling enhanced it somehow? And why had her grandmother refused to believe she was dead?

Did Katie carry the mark of a Timewalker? Sarah hadn't been marked until the Archiver got a hold of her. But if Katie didn't know about the Archiver, how did she know about the Timewalkers and the three day event window?

"Focus, Sarah. We've got to get the hell out of here. If they catch us, we won't get out without killing some of these guys. I really don't want to have to do that."

"Right." Sarah squeezed Tim's hand and pulled more energy into their bodies so they could run faster than they should've been able to. She imagined that she heard the strange chiming rhythm of the Bionic Woman's superpowers kicking in as they moved through the building with super-human speed.

When she wasn't worried about getting millions of people killed or melting bad guy brains, this super-hero thing she had going might actually be kind of fun.

So, she'd be the Bionic Woman. Next, the theme song from the Wonder Woman television show started playing in her head next to a picture of mild-mannered and disguised Katherine Green stepping into a phone booth and magically morphing into the large-busted television star, golden lasso and all.

Wait. Superman used the telephone booth.

Whatever. It was her fantasy, she could play it any way she wanted to.

Katie led them to a secure parking area and motioned them into a dusky gray sedan with windows so darkly tinted they were nearly black. Katie zapped the parking attendant's station so the bar would lift and they cruised through onto the highway in a matter of minutes. Instead of heading out of town as Tim had expected, they headed back toward the city.

"Where are we going?" He held Sarah tightly against him.

Katie hit ninety and kept her tense hands on the steering wheel.

"You'll attract attention going that fast."

Katie shrugged, "They won't touch us. One glance at the license plate and they'll pretend they can't even see us."

"That must come in handy."

"Sometimes." She glanced over at her cousin with a crease in her brow.

"I can feel you buzzing around in my head. Sarah, that's very rude."

Sarah grinned up at him like a guilty three year old before answering. "Sorry, Katie-bug. I just needed to know more about what's going on. How do you know so much about the Timewalkers? And why are you helping us? You know you won't be able to go back now. The Weasel will be hunting for you."

"It doesn't matter. We've been waiting for you to show up for years now."

Tim wanted to break something but focused on keeping his heartbeat steady and his hand wrapped around Sarah's. Being with her was like being on a high-speed roller-coaster with nowhere to get off and no emergency stop button.

She must have felt him tense beneath her because her gaze left her cousin's profile and sought his with a silent apology. She reached up and wrapped her hand around his mark, sending a warm hum of energy through him. Just like that she was forgiven for scaring the shit out of him yet again.

Her fingers caressed his head and neck. If he were a cat he was pretty damn sure he would've started purring. God, this woman drove him crazy.

Katie grinned. "Both of you can just stay out of my head."

"What do you mean, both of you?" These women were all crazy. Why did that thought make him want to smile?

Katie looked at him like he had noodles for brains. "Some of the men begin to take on the skills of their women, especially if they're descendants, too, which you must be to have that mark on your neck."

Ω

Chapter Eleven

Sarah sat up straight and nearly bumped her head against his chin. "How do you know this?"

"The book, Sarah. Grandmother Tilly's book." For the first time since they'd met her, Katie looked truly nervous. "Grandmother left you the book, and a bunch of other stuff. Didn't she ever show it to you?"

"No." Tears gathered in Sarah's eyes, threatening to rip Tim's heart into pieces. Anything but tears.

"Well, we're going to Grandmother Tilly's house. My mother still lives there, guarding it. We've been waiting for the Walker of our time to come. She told us you would come."

"How did she know?" Sarah looked out the window and wiped the tears from her eyes as Katie continued.

"Foresight runs in our line, Sarah. Foresight is one of our gifts."

"Then why the hell don't I have it?"

"I don't know. Why can't I build a storm like you can? I can do what you do on a much smaller scale, but I've got maybe a tenth of your power. Why is that?"

Sarah didn't answer and Katie drove in silence for close to an hour before they pulled into the driveway of a quaint cottage style home obviously built at least one hundred years ago.

Katie shut off the car engine and turned to look Sarah straight in the eye. "Why do you think you were always so good at wind-surfing? You were pushing the wind where you wanted it to go, even then. Then the Archiver got a hold of you and did something to enhance your D.N.A. Now you're a super-hero here to save the world."

Sarah sat in stunned silence and the wind howled outside the vehicle in response to her tentative touch. "Oh, my God. It's true. I never realized."

"Mother and I have been waiting for you for years. Everything is ready. Come on." Katie exited the vehicle, slamming the door closed behind her. She gave them no choice but to follow her to the front door. She didn't knock, just let herself in and left the door open for them to follow her.

Tim held Sarah's hand and entered first, scouting the area and the fiftyish woman waiting for them with her hands in a nervous twist.

Sarah gasped and pulled free of his grasp. "Molly? Is that really you?"

"Yes." The women hugged and smiled, despite the fact that the smiles were filled with pain.

"How much time do you have?"

Tim studied the flickering light that laced the wispy curtains with slices of dawn's first rays. "A little less than twenty-four hours."

Molly nodded and tugged her toward a back room. Sarah gasped and stopped when the energy snapped between them and the pain hit her. Foolish woman. Their connection was stronger now, but she still couldn't go more than a couple feet without repercussions.

"We'll have to work fast." Molly motioned for them to follow. Tim took Sarah's hand and tugged her up against him so he could kiss her. A quick kiss, just to remind her that he was there.

Her smile lit up her eyes and he nearly stumbled when he saw the love shining there. She wasn't trying to hide it, didn't even blink, just stared up at him like he was a god.

Oh, hell yeah. She loved him. Something broken clicked into place inside him. Sure, he'd kill for her, protect her, make love to her every chance he got, but this was more. This was sell-your-eternal-soul-to-the-devil-to-save-her kind of love, something so beyond his scope of experience he couldn't speak. So he kissed her again, longer, deeper, and tried to let her know he'd fight hell itself if he had to. There were no rules he wouldn't break when it came to her. Not anymore.

Molly cleared her throat where she stood in the doorway of what appeared to be a very small bedroom. "Come on, kids, we don't have much time left. We've got to get your flights booked and your ID's finished."

Tim let Sarah pull away from the kiss, but a strange lethargy filled his limbs when she leaned into him and wrapped her arms around his waist. An hour ago he'd been worried the bastard Admiral would kill her. Having her here, in his arms, staring up at him like a love struck teenager was going to his head...and other places.

He had to work to keep his head in the game. Who the hell was Molly, exactly? Why did she have a British accent? And book flights? ID? "What are you talking about? We aren't going anywhere."

"Oh, yes, you are. Grandmother Tilly left explicit

instructions."

Sarah pulled away and led him down the hallway with a gentle tug of her hand at his elbow. "Let me see the book."

"Oh, it's all here for you, Sarah." Molly led Sarah to sit in front of a camera and took her photo, then tugged him into position for his turn.

"What are you doing?" Sarah's puzzled expression spoke for both of them.

"Taking your passport photo, of course." Molly placed an old shoe-box on the quilt covering the small twin bed in the room and headed for the door where Katie waited with a set of car keys. "We've got errands to run, now that you're here. The box contains Grandmother's book, instructions for your travel after the attack on Chicago, and everything she knew or learned about the Timewalkers. Read the book. Get some sleep. We'll be back in a few hours. We'll talk then, okay dear?"

"But how did Gran know?" Sarah's confused face and tapping foot betrayed her nerves.

"*Her* grandmother, Anne, was the first of our line to show up in this time. She arrived in 1864 and stopped two assassination attempts on President Lincoln." With that bombshell, the two women left. The front door slammed seconds later.

"What the hell is going on here, Sarah?"

"I don't know." Sarah stared at the mystery box, then back at him. Sun shown down on it through the window, lighting the container with an unearthly glow. She hesitated, hands shaking, as she sat on the bed and pulled the box onto her lap.

Sarah sat in heart-rending silence.

"Open it." Tim walked over and locked the bedroom door, then sat next to Sarah on the bed. She held the box, unopened, shaking fingers tracing her name written in elegant script on the lid of the box in black marker. "It's her handwriting."

"You okay?"

"I don't know. How could my grandmother do this to me? She knew. She knew and never told me."

"Open the box. Let's find out exactly what she did and didn't know."

A journal lay in tissue paper, plain black leather. Sarah opened it and he peered over her shoulder to see Sarah's name and the mark of the Shen drawn in thick black ink. Sarah turned the page and read aloud.

Dearest Sarah,

I am sorry I couldn't tell you more. I knew you would be Taken from me. I had the vision when you were five years old. Before you get angry, please ask yourself what good would knowing have done you? You would have worried, and cursed your fate instead of living and growing into a healthy and happy human being. I chose not to tell you and I hope you can forgive me. I knew, and I died a little inside each day counting the minutes until you would disappear from my life. I did not want that pain for you.

I must tell you now that I know you will ride the storms, child. And what an amazing gift that is. I have shared dreams with you riding the wind more than once and each time I wake filled with joy. I have also seen the hard-looking soldier destined to be yours. He has a good heart, a bit broken and scarred, but I'm sure your sunshine will heal his soul.

I do not know what your particular mission will entail, so I'm afraid I can't help you with that. I do not know when or where you will have to complete the task the Archiver will assign to you. I know you were always fearless and strong. You are not the type to give up or succumb to defeat, so I have a deep and abiding faith that you will be successful. The only thing I know for sure is that you will find your way home, to this book. I have foreseen you sitting with your soldier reading this book with sunlight in your hair and a heavy heart. I'm sorry, lovebug, but you must leave this city as soon as you are able. There is a Timewalker in need and you must be in place to help her.

My grandmother shared her life with me, and I've placed her story is in these pages. She, too, had the gift of sight. Her story is for another time and is contained in the back of this book for you to read once you are safely on the beach in Bermuda. Her story is interesting, but does not affect the burdens placed on your shoulders. She is simply a fellow sister and traveler through time.

This I know, you will read this book and the following spring a dark haired Timewalker will walk the eastern beach in Bermuda. She will need a sea-worthy boat, money, and your assistance. I do not know her mission or her name, but her mark is on the back of her right shoulder should you desire proof. If you are not able to help her, she will fail in her mission.

I also know that you will need to run, that you will be hunted for your power. So, my child, kill two birds with one stone. Change your name and flee with your soldier to a new home. Do not tell the Archiver what you plan to do. There is a war going on, child, and I've seen some very strange things. Timewalkers and their mates are the only ones you should trust.

I'm sorry I can't tell you more.

Be safe, lovebug. I love you. I'm proud of you. And somewhere in time, I'm holding you in my arms, always.

Love, Granny T

Tears flowed freely down Sarah's face and Tim wrapped her in his arms, absorbing her sobs as she dropped the book to the bed and curled against him.

Hunted for your power.

Yes, the Rear Admiral would never stop looking for her. Right now she was an enigma to him, a strange woman with a bit of power. After the storm, the final battle, she'd be godlike in the Admiral's eyes. A weapon unlike any other. She'd never be safe in the States again. Every camera and software bot out there would be looking for her. Sarah's identity may not have been discovered yet, which could buy them some time, but the Admiral knew him well enough. His home, his money, his identity could all be used like a blood trail to find Sarah.

"Shit." He took the cell phone out of his pocket, pulled the battery out and shoved the mess back in his pocket.

"What are you doing?"

"Disabling the GPS."

"What's GPS?"

"Global Positioning System. It triangulates your position anywhere on Earth using satellites. If I had my phone on, they could track us within a few feet of our position anywhere on the planet."

Sarah shook her head. "I don't belong in this world. In this time. I'm like a three year old, and the things I don't know are going to get you killed."

"No, Sarah. No." He tipped her chin up to look in his eyes. "I know for both of us and I'm not leaving your side." She leaned in and rested her forehead against his, staring into his eyes and straight through to his soul. He hid nothing. "You do your thing tomorrow, you blast that ship out of the sky, and I'll take care of the rest."

She took a slow, deep breath. "Okay."

"Trust me, Sarah. I'll take care of you."

She stopped breathing and he kissed her lightly, coaxing her to relax and draw air back into her body. Letting her go to fend for herself in the world wasn't an option. He could tell her a million reasons why, and they'd all be legitimate, but the truth was he simply refused to let her go. Love meant nothing to him, it was a word he'd used when talking to his mother, when she kissed him after a skinned knee or when he took a head-dive off his bicycle at eleven and broke his wrist. Love was a weak word and didn't begin to encompass what he felt for Sarah, watching her cry, watching as she squared her shoulders time and again to face a terrifying destiny no human should have to face, watching her love him despite his anger at the world, give herself to him despite his ugly ass head and even uglier scars.

Love didn't come close to this obsessive need he had developed to know that she was happy, taken care of, and safe.

He needed her to understand what he felt, to know beyond all doubt, to her very soul, that only death would drag him from her side.

He kissed her again, and with deliberate slowness, he ran his hand up her arm to her collarbone, then her neck and tunneled his fingers beneath the silky strands of her hair. He left a whispered trail of touch against the soft skin beneath his fingertips, and settled his heated palm over the mark there and used the leverage to pull her against him into a fast, furious meeting of lips that spiraled them both instantly into a sensual haze.

The empty box dropped to the floor as he pushed her back and followed her down onto the bed until he covered her delicious body with his own. He was already hard and ready, pressed between her legs exactly where he wanted to be. God he loved how tall she was, how perfectly they fit together when he made love to her, as if she were made for him. And perhaps she had been. He liked the idea of that.

She turned her head to the side in a last ditch effort to restore sanity, but he was having none of it. If he couldn't have her lips, he'd nibble and taste the other bits. They might both be dead in a matter of hours. He had no intention of wasting this opportunity to taste her one more time.

"Tim!" Her panting plea reached his blood starved brain and he stopped.

"Yes?" With a smile he resumed his downward journey and lifted the hem of her shirt out of the way to explore the soft skin of her stomach.

"Shouldn't we be planning battle strategy or something?"

He pulled her shirt over her head and she let him.

"No."

"No? But..."

Tim chuckled and dipped his head to taste the hard pink nipples taunting him with their existence. He kissed his way between them, paying attention to as many lovely freckles as he could, his personal roadmap to heaven.

Sarah wrapped her arms around his head, rubbing the stubble he knew must be there. She pulled his head against her stomach and rubbed against the rough edges of his shaved head with a quick moan and shiver.

I win.

"Hurry up and get naked then." She grinned at him.

"We only have a few hours."

He chuckled and stood to quickly rid himself of his clothes before yanking her shoes and pants off and dumping them into a nice pile with his before covering her completely.

He meant to tease her more, to explore the soft folds of her flesh and make sure she was ready for him, but she reached between them and wrapped her hand around the very tip of his sensitized flesh. He wanted to be inside of her. Now.

He settled for plunging his tongue into her mouth in urgent demand as she placed him right where she wanted him, then tilted her hips up, wrapped her knees around his waist, and impaled herself in one decisive thrust.

Instinct drove him to place his hand over her mark just as the scorching heat of her touch covered his neck. It was like they'd been plugged in to a live wire, energy circling and flowing, one to the other and back in a crescendo that wrapped them up in a vortex of energy, and swirled their souls together in the storm. He couldn't move, couldn't think, could only feel as the energy wound higher and higher, tighter and tighter, until they both cried out in release. He hadn't moved after the initial thrust and he collapsed atop her, buried to the balls and utterly spent.

The energy flowing between them no longer felt like warm, sticky caramel, it was more like floating in a steaming bathtub of hot water. Fluid. Seductive. And completely surrounding them.

She shuddered beneath him and he raised his head, a lovesick grin on his face to find her oh-so-serious and with tears gathering again.

"I can't ask you to give up your life, to move to Bermuda

with me."

"You aren't asking. I'm going." He framed her face in his hands and shifted inside her to remind her of who was in charge now. "You stop the attack. Leave everything else up to me."

"But..."

"No buts, Sarah. Where you go, I go. Forever."

"You'll have to change your name, give up your house, and Bandit, too. What about Bandit?"

"I'm sure Luke and Alexa can take her. She'll be happy with a family around her instead of just a grumpy old soldier like me for company."

"But..."

"No buts. I am yours." He pulled her wrist up until she took the hint and put her hand over his mark once more. "And you are mine." Turning her head to the side with a gentle nudge of his finger, he nuzzled her neck and placed a kiss over her mark. Instantly the connection hummed back to life and he felt himself harden within her. She moaned and shifted beneath him, taking him deeper, reigniting the flame in both of them.

"But, Tim..."

He was done arguing. He covered her mouth with his own and didn't let her up for air until she was done fighting him.

A couple hours later, Sarah finally slept, curled next to him under the homemade quilt she'd told him her grandmother had made for her room when she was twelve. It was covered in dancing butterflies and exquisite stitching so detailed the creatures looked like they would fly off at any time. He set the alarm in his watch and drifted to sleep, with

Sarah in his arms.

When he woke he knew two things, Katie couldn't come with them when they left here, and Sarah had been keeping secrets.

Ω
Chapter Twelve

Thursday, 10:24 A.M.

Ten in the morning. He had less than twenty hours to figure a way out of this mess or Sarah was going to die.

Tim walked slowly down the hallway and followed the light and smell of hot coffee to the small kitchen. Two sober faces waited with a map and a stack of paperwork beside them.

"Have a seat, Tim. I'd offer you whiskey if I had it, but I don't."

"Coffee is great. Thanks." He sat in the chair across from Katherine and studied her face. Now that Sarah was asleep, the women didn't try to hide their worry.

"What the hell is going on, Katie? I just had a vision with two possible outcomes."

Katie nodded but didn't say anything, just stared into her own cup. It was the elder cousin, Molly, who answered. "We call it a Time Crux, a moment where more than one outcome is possible."

"Okay, well in one of them, Sarah dies. Tell me how to make sure that doesn't happen."

"I'm sorry. We can't." Katie twisted her mug in circles and shook her head. "If it's a Time Crux it means she hasn't made the decision yet."

"What decision? In both visions she was battling the freak storm over Chicago, and winning. Then, in the first parallel she just... dies."

Tim hadn't shed a tear in years, but he found he had to wipe his face with the back of his hand in front of these two women and their pitying stares.

Molly covered his hand with a warm, motherly touch and waited for him to look her in the eyes, eyes strikingly similar to Sarah's. "There's nothing you can do, Tim. The moment will come, and whatever is going to happen will happen. It might be Sarah's decision, and it might be the decision of someone else. But the person who is the cause of the Crux will have to choose."

"Bullshit. I don't believe there's nothing I can do. And who is this other person? How do I find them?"

"Did you have a sense of what she was battling, or what she was thinking about during either parallel of the vision?"

"No."

"Then you're just going to have to wait and see. The moment will come. The decision might be hers, yours, or someone else's entirely. It could be a firefighter on the ground, or the Admiral deciding to help or hinder her. There is, quite simply, no way to know until the moment arrives." Molly withdrew her hand and leaned back in her chair, lines of sorrow etched in her face. "I'm so sorry."

Tim wanted to explode, but there was no outlet for his rage. Bullshit. Bullshit. Bullshit. He'd take her away from here, keep her off that damn tower, get the hell out of Chicago...

No, he wouldn't. Even if he could force himself to sacrifice the lives of nine million innocent civilians, which he couldn't and knew it, she'd never agree to go.

"Okay. So, what can I do?"

"Sign these." Katie slid a stack of legal documents across the table with a blue pen lying across the top. "This is your Last Will and Testament dated three weeks after your parents' deaths. It leaves everything you own to your long lost cousin and his wife, John T. Davis and Mary S. Davis. They are U.S. citizens who live in Bermuda, but happen to be in Chicago right now on vacation. They're due to return home in the next three days."

Tim picked up the pen and stared blankly at the documents. "What?"

Katie kept talking and dumped the contents of a small white Tyvek envelope on the table. "Here are your new birth certificates, identification, and passports. You are now John Timothy Davis, married to one Mary Sarah Davis. Here are your tickets. We've chartered a jet that will take you to Bermuda in the morning. The pilot is one of us, so there will be no questions. The flight is scheduled to leave at 9:05 AM, so we will have about three hours to get you to the airport once Sarah is finished with the attack."

Tim leafed through the documents before him. Simple, straightforward, and the will named Molly June Higgins, Esquire the executor of his estate. He looked at Molly in surprise. "You're an attorney?"

"Yes. I've had these papers drawn up and waiting for the details for years. When Sarah disappeared, Granny T called me in London and begged me to move back home. My husband was gone. I was a widow with nothing to lose. Besides, once she'd shown me the book and the journal of the first Walker in our line, what else could I do but believe her?"

Molly blushed, but continued, "Besides, I have a touch of the visions myself. There's no denying that, is there, son?"

Katie nodded beside her. "We were careful, Tim. We knew you'd need to get out of here, and thanks to Tilly, and we've had years to prepare. We've been waiting. Mom's last name is different from mine. I covered my tracks. The Rear Admiral thinks I was abandoned by a crack addicted teen at the hospital and grew up a ward of the state of Illinois in the foster care system. I've got all the records to prove it, thanks to some well-placed friends. He'll never suspect a thing."

"How the hell did you two pull this off? How many Timewalkers are out there wandering around?"

"Timewalkers as powerful as Sarah? None that we know of." Katie raised her mug in salute. "But weaker descendants, like me? We don't know for sure, but there are over twenty cousins in our family line, descendants of Anne, and we all have a bit of the gifts. We've found several more and placed them in the Casper Project under the Rear Admiral. He doesn't know who they really are, he just wants their power."

Tim digested that bit of information then pointed out the obvious. "One problem, ladies. I'm not dead."

Katie rubbed her hands together and actually grinned. "You will be. We've got it all planned out. All I need is an hour of your time. We're going to the dentist."

Tim thumbed through everything, the will, identification, passports. His whole life...*erased* by what lay on the table in front of him.

He thought of the woman asleep in the room down the hall and signed his Last Will and Testament with a flourish of blue ink. Reaching into his pocket, he pulled out a key and wrote down an address and instructions. He slid the key and paper to Molly. She scanned it with a smile.

"Not a problem, Tim. I can take care of this. Katie can give it all to you once you're safely on the plane."

"Can we get my dog into the country? I don't want to leave her behind. Luke and Alexa have her right now." He wrote down Luke's cell phone number and tried not to smile at their obvious excitement. He'd just handed them a prize, another female to torture with questions and pull into their machinations. Although, their network of descendants was about to save him and Sarah a lot of trouble. He was grateful and willing to do whatever it took to help them make it happen.

Katie leaned forward eagerly, nearly spilling her coffee. "Alexa? From San Antonio?"

Tim shrugged. "I don't know."

"Lawson?"

"Yes. That's her husband's name."

Katie beamed. "I knew it! I knew she was a Timewalker." She turned to her mother. "She's the one who caught that colonel's crazy son before he released that nasty virus. Luke Lawson. I knew there was a reason the Rear Admiral wanted him watched. I suspected she was one of us. I can't wait to meet her."

"You better tell him he's under surveillance."

"Oh, I will! I've been covering her tracks for a couple of weeks now. I had a feeling..." Katie trailed off, obviously going somewhere he didn't need to follow.

Tim smiled and imagined Luke's groan of pain when the ladies all got together and started their storytelling. He'd be on the beach and Luke would be swimming in a pool of time traveler estrogen. He rubbed his hands together. "Okay, ladies. Fill me in. How am I going to die?"

* * *

Friday, 4:56 AM

Sarah stared out the window of black sedan and let Tim drive her through the darkened city streets. He left her to her thoughts now, simply held her hand. He was there. Live or die, he was with her, and that was more than she had a right to ask for.

But she'd take it anyway. He'd pulled her back from the brink before, when she'd been chasing the young girl's energy through the storm. But since they'd made love at Molly's house her energy patterns had changed. She didn't constantly buzz with painful trickles of power. She floated in it like a baby in a warm bath. Somehow, Tim pulled the pain away, organized the energy and let her access it when she wanted to, instead of having the universe shoving barbed wire down her throat.

They'd discussed the possible options with Katie before leaving the house. Katie agreed with her that she needed to be out in the open, preferably next to the water where she'd have access to the city's power grid on one side and the total kinetic energy of Lake Michigan and the windy turmoil of air currents on the other. Tim suggested they go back to the rooftop of the Hancock Observatory, that way both the city's electrical supply and the natural elements would be accessible. She'd have access to massive amounts of power if she needed it, or knew what the hell to do with it. That was the rub, she still had no idea what this attack was going to be like or how to fight it.

Tim had poured over Luke's flash drive for hours looking for information. There was a bunch of theoretical physics and quantum theory there. Math. Like she could do equations as she battled the attack she knew was coming. But he'd sorted through it with his analytical mind, furious that someone had managed to salvage his initial ideas and theories and twist them into ideas for a weapon of mass destruction. But at least he had a couple working theories.

The first was a frontal attack with some kind of fire molecule, something actually burning. She was pretty sure she could handle that.

The second theory was a redirected solar flare. If these aliens had somehow managed to collect the energy from solar flares and direct it at Chicago, that might be a bit more of a challenge.

The third idea was some kind of magnetic weapon that created super-particles that would react with and incinerate anything they came into contact with.

That one scared the shit out of her, so she figured that would be the lucky winner.

And what about the young girl's strange energy? She could still feel it, had pulled Katie and Molly into a psychic link, and even they had recognized the resonating hum in their souls. This girl was not a Timewalker. She was something else, something more than that.

And she was here, somewhere. Young, vulnerable, and trusting Sarah to take care of these bastards today.

Yeah, no pressure.

"Hey, how you holding up? You okay?" Tim pulled her hand to his mouth and kissed her fingertips, then the back of her hand as he parked the car. They had about ten minutes until dawn.

She studied the outline of his stubborn jaw, his firm

mouth and regal nose, the intelligent predatory gleam in his eyes as they focused exclusively on her in what could be their final minutes together.

Timewalkers had failed in the past. The black plague, the holocaust and both world wars. Epic failures. Millions of dead.

Just because she had the mark didn't mean she was going to win. Sometimes, the good guys lost.

Tim's hawk-like features narrowed and he pulled her across the seat until they were nose-to-nose, sharing breath. Sharing life.

"I love you, Timothy Daniel Tucker." She leaned forward and brushed a chaste kiss on his lips. It tasted of her tears.

"I love you, Sarah." He kissed her quickly, a brief punishing kiss. "You annihilate this thing and let's get the hell out of here."

Sarah nodded, kissed his cheek, and tried to pull away, but he stopped her. Confused, she waited for him to say whatever seemed to be caught in his throat.

"Sarah, promise me you'll fight for me, for us. Promise me you'll come back to me."

The grim set of his mouth and the sadness in his gaze made her want to weep. "I promise I'll fight with everything I've got."

"We win together or we die together, Sarah." The truth of that statement crippled her tongue. There was no room for argument in his emotions or his tone. "Where you go, I go."

Unable to speak past the lump in her chest, she nodded and placed her hand over his mark to enjoy one last moment of warm comfort before she entered hell on earth.

The hair on the back of her neck rose and she felt like ice

cubes were being rubbed over every inch of her skin. The enemy had arrived. "It's time."

She yanked away from him and got out of the car to face the rising wind currents coming off the water, racing through the city streets like cold snakes seeking prey.

They raced for the doorway to the Hancock Observatory, and she blasted past the locks and into the elevator with Tim hot on her heels. The elevator ride seemed to take hours, but only a few minutes passed before she ran for the rooftop, bursting onto the top of the tower as a roiling cloud of orange and red light rumbled across the water toward the city. The cloud hid the alien ship, she was sure of it. The attack would come from there.

"Tim!" She glanced over her shoulder searching for him. He was right behind her, less than a foot away. "You're here."

"Always." She smiled at him, every ounce of love she had for him bursting through her cells like champagne bubbles. He smiled back and settled his hands on her hips, taking up position behind her. "You go take out that fucking thing. Kill it. I've got you and I'm never letting go."

Turning, she raised her arms to the sky and opened herself to the flow of energy around the city. Pressure built inside her body as the alien ship's power built a charge in the sky above them, pushing at her with an invisible fist until she couldn't move enough to draw breathe. She felt like a soda bottle, shaken, waiting for that one little tap to explode her into a million foaming bubbles.

She leaned her head back to rest on Tim's shoulder and focused her gaze to the northern sky where the mass of brilliant lights gained speed and momentum in the clouds.

She contemplated shooting out at it like a missile, but

instead left her frail human form in Tim's care and floated up into the air. She allowed her will, her conscious power to expand beneath the cloud formation and tried to form a giant safety net for the city.

She could feel it now, the narrow energy band the alien ship operated within. It felt slightly off, somehow out of synch with this reality. Disharmonious, like a C sharp that didn't belong in the middle of a song.

That discordant note shimmered in the air all around her, coming from the cloud. There was no distinct mass she could attack, no ship she could detect, just a giant sense of wrongness that grated on every nerve she had like fingernails on a chalkboard.

Then it simply stopped and an eerie silence took its place, a silence no one else would be able to hear. It was as if all the energy around them had been sucked into an invisible black hole, like there was nothing left to notice, like the sky, the wind, the clouds no longer existed at all.

Like she was out of time.

She was *outside* of the time stream...

Sarah nearly lost herself in the pull of that nothingness, the void in reality that opened up above her. Only Tim's presence kept her sane, let her know she existed in this empty place.

It could have been seconds or centuries before the cold nothingness expanded like a percussion blast from a nuclear weapon and the whole world went black. There was nothing but a few pinpoints of light, like tiny pieces of glitter stuck in a sea of black tar. A few hundred tiny specks flickered with light in her awareness and she clung to the sensation of Tim's hands on her hips, his heat at her back. She couldn't feel them, not really, but she knew they were there.

That knowing kept her calm as the energy wave raced over her now, a malignant consciousness stopped to inspect her, then moved on to the next tiny sparkle of light, and the next. She looked down to where her heart would have been and discovered that one of the flickering lights, one of the brightest lights in this strange timeless darkness, belonged to her soul.

Her attention snapped up and she followed the creature, the evil ooze that had touched her. It raced from light to light, like a snake waiting to devour the waiting souls whole.

The alien life force moved faster than her mind could track, searching for something. Or someone...

She felt herself smile and looked down again, the young girl's energy pattern was still safely hidden within her own, a soul wrapped in a soul, shielded and protected from detection. Her ruse, her near loss of life, had worked.

The knowledge filled her with satisfaction and she reinforced the web of light and lies she had woven around the young girl's soul, offering further protection.

The light fought to be free, to shine beside hers and she realized that hundreds of tiny threads were weaving and crawling toward her, making their way through this nowhere space, instinctively reacting to her presence. They were all linked together...and leading the serpentine coldness straight to her vulnerable soul.

And the aliens wanted her dead.

Ω
Chapter Thirteen

Friday, 5:17 AM

Sarah wrapped her energy around the girl and pulled on the life threads of every Timewalker descendant on Earth. They were the lights in the darkness. There were hundreds, all linked to potential power. She crushed the girl's energy into a tiny light and surrounded it with the mass of energy she pulled from the other Walkers until the monsters that stalked them all became confused and withdrew completely, leaving this strange place behind like its twisted shadow.

Too late she realized her mistake. If it couldn't kill the girl here, in the energy fields, it would eliminate her frail human body, burn to death the human girl they hunted on Earth. They'd burn Chicago to the ground to ensure the girl's physical body could not survive.

They'd kill her here, or Chicago would burn.

She lost either way. If she left the girl here alone, linked to the other Timewalker descendants like a homing beacon, the alien consciousness would crush her. If she pulled away to fight the physical attack on Chicago, the girl's energy would be vulnerable to attack here.

Chicken or egg.
Body or soul.
Dead or dead.

She covered the girl's energy the best she could and raced back to her waiting body, to Tim on the rooftop and a glorious fall of silvery ash that appeared out of thin air and floated down toward the city. Maybe she could do both...

She'd do it or die trying. God, she loved Tim, and she really didn't want to die, but the mission came first.

Burying the girl's soul inside her own now, linked to all the others, pulled the energy fabric of the Earth plane into a strange pretzel that would be absolutely impossible to hide for long from the cold consciousness hunting her.

The explosion she'd felt in the energy field was absent here on Earth. Instead of chaos and aftershocks knocking her off her feet, she felt nothing but an odd and peaceful silence as the glittering mass of silver flakes floated down like a light dusting of snow. It was infinitely more beautiful and more deadly than any snowstorm could be.

Sarah reached for them with her mind, trying to feel them, to neutralize them and drain them of their power.

They parted before her, pushed away by a magnetic force of opposites. She was of this world, they were other. Their energy spun backward, away from her, impossible for her to touch or control.

She had listened to Tim explain what he knew about magnetics and theoretical physics. They'd been right and wrong. These particles would burn Chicago to the ground, not with fire or explosions, but with millions of tiny incinerations as they collided with the matter of *this* world, the energy of this world, *this* reality's electron particles spun in the opposite direction of those in the tiny attacking particles of light.

The opposite of light was not dark, it was light that

existed in the opposite direction. These aliens were crossing boundaries never meant to be crossed, twisting existence itself into a warped backward world. Dark and light can't occupy the same space. Up can't be down. Reality and non-reality literally can't co-exist in the same space.

Pull them back into the void, Sarah.

Tim's suggestion flooded her mind with confidence and she realized he'd been with her all along. His confident voice filled her left ear as they stared at the mass together. "It came from that place. Its energy signature will be drawn back to it if we can just open the door for it to go home."

The cold nothingness wouldn't explode or burn. There was no time, no life, no buildings, people, or earth for it to burn. It wasn't conscious. It had no life force or intelligence of its own. The glittering power of the silver storm was magnetic and growing at an exponential rate as every molecule it bumped into changed its energy pattern to match the storm. She could feel each collision costing the particles power, but they wouldn't die soon enough. They'd grow in numbers until they incinerated Chicago, and probably three to four feet of Earth beneath her, before they lost enough charge to become harmless dust.

But the void had nothing to burn, it had nothing at all.

Pull it into the void.

Tim forced the thought into her mind and she steeled her will to control the energy she'd need to twist open the pretzel in space-time she had around herself and pull them through. Or force them through.

Sarah leaned into him, aware now of his consciousness entwined with hers in the field of energy surrounding them. "I'll try."

And she did. But nothing moved. She could pull energy and move it around, had created a chaotic swirl of wind and lightning over Lake Michigan, but the vortex the weapon had created is what had pulled her into its reality the first time, and the enemy had firmly closed that door once their weapon had been launched through it.

So, the light of her soul, of the girl's, and all the Timewalker descendants were still there, visible, stuck in that place of cold, inky darkness.

Sarah flung her consciousness and every ounce of will she possessed into her storm, trying to force, push, pull or draw the deadly glitter away from the city and reopen that door. She couldn't do it.

"Tim!" She needed help, she needed something she could feel in the back of her mind, in *his* mind. Knowledge. Understanding of the time strands and the nature of reality itself.

"Let me in, Sarah." Tim shouted the command as a bolt of lightning slashed the antennae behind them and they were covered in a brilliant shower of sparks.

Let me in. Give me the storm.

They had seconds before the deadly particles would reach the tops of the buildings. Seconds until death.

Sarah surrendered everything, opened herself completely to Tim. No secrets, no hiding. Everything was laid bare for him to see, her fear, her determination, and her love for him. He could destroy her now, but she didn't care. She gave him access to her power. Gave him the small light she hid and trusted him to help her protect it. Gave him her soul, and had faith that he'd return it to her in one piece.

His spirit floated in beside her, filling her from the inside out, merging them into one mind with one goal.

She'd expected calm from him, cold determination and analytical strategies or theories to be running through his head like a machine.

Instead she was engulfed in a cold fire, an inferno of rage that this thing would dare threaten his world, his woman.

He was angry that this thing would destroy *her*. It was personal and fierce. The last thread of control she'd been holding snapped and she shoved everything she had into him, pulled power from the wind currents, the earth beneath her feet, the constant barrage of waves and water crashing in the lake. The buildup of power was enormous, and still he needed more. Lightning flashed across the sky in giant webs of her will, surrounding them in a deafening battle of sound that shook the building and reverberated through her chest like a bomb blast. She stopped thinking and became the weapon Tim needed to wield to save them. She would have lost her feet, but Tim's solid stance behind her held their bodies in place as they battled the invisible enemy on the other side of the void.

They were watching, she could feel the sick oily stain of their malignant minds moving around the light of her soul, sniffing like rabid wolves at a piece of fresh meat. A chill raced through her, not a physical cold, nothing so innocent as that. This cold would drain her, send her heart and mind into an abyss of darkness so profound she'd never find her way out. The cold penetrated her defenses and crawled through her awareness like cold sludge moving through her body, chilling her and stealing her will to fight.

She pushed it back with more power from the Earth mother, the animals, the wind and rain and rocking water of the oceans. She expanded her consciousness until she was no longer human, no longer Sarah, but part of the universe itself.

And still the chilling cold pulled at the edges of her mind.

Tim!

I feel it.

Sarah dove into his thoughts and saw his plan. He knew how to fight this thing, he understood it in a way she could not, in formulas and mathematical theories that existed in his mind, making these things concrete, real, and stealing their invincibility from them.

He knew where they were. He understood what they did and how they moved through reality, through time.

He could find them, he just needed the power to get to them, to open the door.

Sarah pulled more, felt the tiny soul huddled within her own fight with her, calling on the link she had with all the Timewalkers, Sarah drew them all into the fight. All their minds, their skills and energies. All their wills merged for an infinite moment in time into one will, one mind, one soul.

Katie was there, and Molly, Alexa and Luke. Those energies she recognized. But there were scores more, minds tuned to the call, souls that answered and fed her the power and control that she needed to help Tim do the impossible and command the door between worlds.

Force it open, and force this nasty death dust back to where it came from.

The energy built inside her, around her, until she was the center of a hurricane of invisible energy that would make a nuclear bomb look like a firecracker in the rain. The aliens wouldn't need to destroy Chicago. If she didn't get the energy under control they'd blow half of North America off the map.

"Tim!" She screamed it at him, body and mind, and tore through his barriers to his bare mind, forcing him to funnel the power, to twist it to his own ends.

His thoughts silenced, calm and cold as a machine as his mind raced to comprehend and hold the incomprehensible. No human mind could cleave to the knowledge he now commanded, no mere human could withstand the rush of electromagnetic energy flowing through them.

"We're more than human, Sarah." Tim smiled and stepped up beside her, pulled her raised arm down and entwined their fingers. His meaning drifted between them and the hundreds of connected souls feeding them power, understanding and will. "We always were."

Sarah squeezed his hand and nodded as they stood quiet and still in the eye of the storm. She kept the energy raging, throwing dust and debris into the air to interact with the *other* particles, slowing their fall and stealing their power in tiny increments.

The twisted lines of reality that were torqued and folded around her uncurled in response to Tim's directed energy and will. He knew it existed. He understood it, and that gave him the power to open the doorway between worlds.

"Just a crack, Sarah. Any more and we could destroy everything, or worse, let more of this stuff in."

She nodded and fed him the power he needed.

The moment reality shifted, the discordant notes of power shooting from that tiny rift in reality screamed through her like a police siren inside her head. It hurt like hell. She fell to her knees beside Tim, hand still clasped in his as massive amounts of energy flowed between them.

Tim focused on holding the door open, the crushing

weight of two realities threatening to buckle their combined will despite the massive amounts of power she gave him to command.

"Now, Sarah."

She had to summon the particles, she had to become the sound in her head, a giant magnet to attract them back home.

She wrapped her energy around that non-sound in her mind, the scream of wrongness in her soul and sent it out to ride the wind, to settle over the particles of this world like masks, fooling the *other,* drawing them to her in a river of dark matter streaming toward her.

She couldn't allow the pieces of this world through the doorway, so she called them to her, then tore the offending energy signature from them at the last moment.

The song of their home dimension pulled the particles through the door and a small river of beautiful shimmering death vanished into thin air in the space a few feet in front of them.

A giant vacuum of nothing existed in their wake and normal matter rushed in to fill the space with a sonic boom of sound. Shattering glass from hundreds of office windows filled the city as the doorway between worlds collapsed.

The repercussion hit their minds with the force of a sledgehammer and Sarah fell to her knees next to Tim as her vision went black.

* * *

Tim woke with Sarah in his arms and the rumble of jet engines in his ears. They were laid out together on a makeshift bed of blankets and pillows on the floor of a six-seater jet.

He looked around and found Katie sitting nearby, a

watchful and worried expression on her face as she stared at Sarah's unconscious face.

"We made it?"

"You made it." Katie's smile was filled with relief and the aftershocks of terror he was sure they were all going to be feeling for a long time.

"Am I dead?"

Katie set his duffel bag beside him on the floor then resumed her seat and clapped her hands together in front of her face. "Do you want the good news or the bad news first?"

Tim sighed and hugged Sarah tighter. "Surprise me."

"You are very, very dead, Timothy Daniel Tucker. We planted your cell phone up there, so we got you a new one. It's in the bag. And we got Bandit on board."

"Good." He couldn't go back. Ever. Luke's flash drive held all the proof he needed to know that they were already twisting his work to their own ends at the government labs. He didn't know who had stolen his work, or when they'd managed to sneak in and copy his private notes, but he wasn't really surprised. Now he had his research, his money, and the few personal items he'd hidden away. "And the bad news?"

Katie's grim face set free a colony of bees in his gut. "Luke and Alexa are off grid. Their house was destroyed by the Triscani right after the attack this morning."

"Shit."

"Yours was, too." Her grin was forced. "We'll forward Mr. Davis the insurance check."

His house? Gone? "What about Molly? Your house? It sounds like they are tracking Sarah." His head spun with the implications. A life on the run. Had they found a way to track her? Or were they having an aliens' version of a temper tantrum since they'd gotten their asses kicked this morning by the beautiful Mrs. Davis?

"Our house is fine. I don't know how they knew about your house or Alexa's, but there's been no sign of them at all around mom's house. And since this morning, we'd know."

That was true enough. Every Timewalker descendant on Earth had been pulled into that battle with them. They'd all felt the strange energy and malevolent touch of the Triscani's world.

To hell with them. If the bad guys tried to come after them, so be it. He and Sarah would take them down as many times as it took. The Triscani had to know that he wouldn't run from a fight. Not with them. Fucking bastards.

He buried his nose in Sarah's hair and let the future flow over him in a warm haze. Sarah on the beach under the hot sun, a cold drink in her hand and a tiny bikini barely covering her delicious body. His. Forever.

"Wake up, Mrs. Davis." He ordered Sarah to come to. He needed to know she was all right, that the cold darkness he'd felt trying to devour her was well and truly gone.

Katie smiled in understanding. "You've both been out for a few hours. But all of her vitals were fine, so she should wake up any time." She stood and tugged her jacket into place, ever the professional. "I'll just go have a chat with the pilot and give you some time to adjust. We'll be in Bermuda in a couple of hours. We've got Bandit up front. She's keeping my uncle company."

She walked to the cockpit and a heavily accented British voice drifted through the plane before she closed the door behind her, leaving him alone with Sarah.

He tightened his arms around her in what he knew would be a painful grip, but couldn't stop his need to feel her, alive and warm in his arms. Silent tears defied his orders and slid into her hair.

That *thing* they'd face had scared the living shit out of him. It was not good or evil, not dark or light, it was...nothing. A cold, alien nothing that would swallow the world whole and still not be satisfied.

And Sarah had faced it and not flinched. She'd battled it and defied it, denied it the souls it wanted to consume, the souls that stood in its way. Without the light, the Triscani invaders would be free to erase everything. The Timewalkers were the army in their path, defending existence simply by being, by fighting, by refusing to give up even in the face of overwhelming odds.

And he was one of them. He'd felt the call of the strands that wrapped around this reality, this stream of time that cradled them and their world.

If it were to unravel, their world would cease to exist.

His little experiments, his obsession with Nikola Tesla, were now insignificant in the face of this cold reality.

The darkness would stop at nothing to reach that little girl's light still cradled inside Sarah's soul, inside his own. They both covered her now, fought her stubborn, childlike desire to be free from their temporary cage.

He sent the child his tears, his pain at nearly losing Sarah and the full scope of terror, the absolute power over dark energies that the enemy hunting her had at its command.

The girl settled, defiant but not quite ready to face what he'd shown her. Sarah wouldn't approve. She wanted to coddle the girl, surround her with love and warmth, to teach her humanity and compassion. Tim had to hope her parents, whoever and whatever they were, would take care of that. His job now, his and Sarah's job, was to keep that little light hidden until she was grown.

The child had caused the Crux. She'd had to decide, during the fight, whether to live and be hunted, or slide away in peace.

The girl had hesitated as she battled her fear of the dark ones. He'd felt it, known that if the girl had chosen to leave and be reborn in another era, as she'd done in the past, that Sarah would have died trying to save her, trying to convince her to fight.

The child was a not a Timewalker, but they fought for her. He'd let her see the courage Sarah displayed while fighting for her survival, for the survival of millions, and hoped the child would rise to the occasion. She had, but that didn't mean she could come out of hiding. She was still small. Still young. And they had no idea who she was or how to find her. So, he had to scare her a little. And that meant letting her see the monster that waited for her so she'd stop trying to get out of the cage.

"Stop scaring her."

"She needs to be scared. Otherwise she'll do something foolish."

"Like what?"

"Oh, I don't know." He kissed her temple. "Like throw lightning bolts at aliens from the top of tall buildings?"

"Hmm. Sounds like my kind of girl."

Tim laughed and turned Sarah, and her smart mouth, to face him. "Exactly what I'm afraid of."

Sarah smiled and reached for him, wrapped her arm

around his head, around his mark, and pulled his lips to hers. He kissed her tenderly, grateful for the love that hummed between them in a current more electric and powerful than anything else in the universe.

"We made it." Tears slid down her cheeks and dripped onto his arm which she was currently using as a pillow.

"We made it."

"Are you dead?"

"Yes. Katie and Molly took care of it. I didn't ask where they got the bodies, but the police will find Tim Tucker and an unknown female burned to cinders at the top of the Hancock Observatory, presumably hit by lightning during a freak storm."

"Nice way to go."

"I thought so."

Sarah pushed him onto his back and curled into his side like a sleepy kitten. He couldn't blame her, he still felt like he'd been run over by a half mile of back-to-back semi trucks.

"Now to the beach?"

"To the beach, a little cottage and a dive-shop owned by Mr. and Mrs. Davis."

"That will be nice. I love the beach."

He pulled her tightly against his side and reached into his duffel bag. When he had what he needed, he pulled Sarah's hand up to his chest and slid his grandmother's diamond and emerald engagement ring onto her finger.

"Mrs. Davis, will you marry me?"

Sarah froze, then rose onto one elbow to kiss him until he was out of breath and desperate to hear her answer. Her mission was over. She had control of her power without touching him now. She didn't need him anymore, not even to protect the child. He could and would help her with that from afar if he had to, and she would know that. The child knew it and had maintained her connection to them both.

The thought of Sarah out there alone, making her way in the world without him, cut him deeply inside where no one could see him bleed. "I love you, Sarah. Say yes."

Sarah slid the ring all the way down her finger and made a fist to keep it there. "I love you, and your scars, and your freaky math brain."

"Is that a yes?"

"Yes." She kissed his forehead. "Yes." Her lips grazed his cheek.

"Definitely, yes." Soft feminine lips covered his with a promise he'd never once thought he'd find in a woman's kiss...forever.

And with a Timewalker, no telling just how long that might be.

Timewalker Chronicles Book 2: Silver Storm

An excerpt...

Timewalker Chronicles, Book 3:
Ω
BLUE ABYSS
By Michele Callahan

Challenger Bank, West of Bermuda, Northern Tip of the Bermuda Triangle.

Something urged her on, called to her...something she couldn't explain and had given up fighting. Mari released more spool line and kept swimming, leaving the mercenary she'd hired behind her in the dark silence of the underwater caves they explored.

Yes, there had been a time in her life when all things made perfect sense. It felt a lifetime ago, when she'd been sure of herself, safe in her understanding of the world around her. But that was *before*, before the long nights studying, the lonely hours poring over images and scouring the internet for something, anything, that could explain her bizarre dreams and help her discover the truth.

She'd spent hours investigating Roswell on foot, looking for evidence and inspiration in equal measure. She'd found nothing to help her there, had been forced to widen her net beyond the infamous 'hot spots' of alien activity. Roswell? Nothing. Area 51? Total bust. She'd chased them all. Atlantis. The northern lights. Mayan ruins. The pyramids.

Anything unusual, suspicious, or even remotely possible

had her hopping on a jet armed with her laptop, an almost anthropology degree, a paranoid religious upbringing that often spoke of "demons"…which sounded a lot like very nasty inter-dimensional beings to her…and her dreams, the never-ending nightmares that no one else in the world could ever hope to comprehend.

What was hell anyway, if not another dimension? One she feared and chased with identical fervor.

She was now a laughingstock in her extended family, a college drop-out, a rumor chasing freak, and a joke of monumental proportions in her home town of Santa Fe. She had lost her parents to an eighteen-wheeler in a blizzard, her brother to meth, and then half of her inheritance chasing answers.

Strange beings. Secret languages. Travelers who left their mark on our world? According to the masses, it was all nonsense, the stuff of wild conspiracy theorists. Her mother, God rest her soul, had crossed herself and spent hours bent over the rosary many, many nights. And every night that young Mari had woke screaming, she prayed until the sun rose. Her father, the surgeon, was plagued with guilt that he couldn't heal his own daughter. So, he used to sit her down with a homemade croissant, still warm from the oven and drizzled with chocolate sauce. She'd nibbled the confection while he read stories to her through all hours of the night. Neither prayer nor chocolate had helped stop the dreams, nor provided any answers. Nothing had.

Until now….

Blue Abyss – Available May 2014

Join my New Release Alerts e-mail list @ http:www.michelecallahan.com (Just New Release E-mails...Nothing Else)

Books by Michele Callahan

Timewalker Chronicles:
RED NIGHT
SILVER STORM
BLUE ABYSS (May 2014)
BLACK GATE (June 2014)
WHITE FIRE (August 2014)

The Chimera Series:
CHIMERA BORN (June 2014)
Coming Soon – Chimera's Kiss

The Ozera Wars:
ROGUE'S DESTINY
QUEEN'S DESTINY
WARRIOR'S DESTINY
Coming Soon – Hunter's Destiny

MICHELE CALLAHAN

Timewalker Chronicles: Red Night
Copyright © 2011 by Michele Callahan
Cover design © 2014 by RomCon®

Timewalker Chronicles: Silver Storm
Copyright © 2012 by Michele Callahan
Cover design © 2014 by RomCon®

Blue Abyss Copyright © 2014 by Michele Callahan
All rights reserved.

These books are works of fiction. Names, people, places and events are completely a product of the authors imagination or used fictitiously. Any resemblance to any persons, living or dead, is completely coincidental.

No part of this book may be reproduced or copied in any form or format, by electronic, digital, or mechanical means including, but not limited to, information storage and retrieval systems, without written permission from Michele Callahan. An exception is granted to book reviewers who may quote up to 250 words in a review.

Thank you very much for honoring the hours of hard work each author puts into a story.

http://www.michelecallahan.com
http://www.romcon.com

About The Author:

Michele Callahan is a wife, mother, romance and science fiction addict, and founder of RomCon, the only Fan Convention geared toward women who read romance and genre fiction. Suffering from a healthy case of sci-fi/fantasy fever, Michele never turns down an opportunity to sit through a Star Wars, True Blood, Game of Thrones, LOTR, or Matrix marathon.

Her favorite things in books; hot heroes, superpowers, freakish things that can't be explained by modern science, and true love! Her past jobs include fast-food drive through goddess, nurse's aide, cashier, anatomy & physiology instructor, medical office nurse, and entrepreneur. When she's at home her life is ruled by her family plus two 100 pound rescue dogs and their wagging tails (which should really be classified as dangerous weapons.)

Her all-time favorite movie list includes: The Matrix, Terminator, Star Wars – The Empire Strikes Back, The Princess Bride, Braveheart, and Jerry Maguire. (BTW- She doesn't understand that list either…)

You can contact Michele via e-mail:

Michele (at) michelecallahan.com.

Dear Reader,

My beloved friend, CJ Snyder, passed away in 2013 after a painful and courageous battle with breast cancer. I miss her every single day. I do what I can to honor her memory.

That is my intention in sharing the following excerpt with you. She was my best friend, a kind and loving spirit, and one hell of a great writer. Thank you for reading, and for helping me to keep her books, and her amazing gift, alive.

Michele

Excerpt:
While You Were Dead

A Thrill-Ride of Romantic Suspense by CJ Snyder

Prologue

Twelve years ago...

Kat Jannsen didn't cry the day they buried Maxwell Crayton.

Plenty of others did. Mourners gathered four and five deep around the long, flag-draped coffin. Even more had packed the church, but Kat skipped the God part.

She stayed back by a tree, feeling out of place, uninvited, unwelcome and wondering about the flag. Military? What other secrets had he kept?

Kat couldn't say why she'd come. Except she'd loved him, as she'd never loved another human being in her life. So much hope about to be buried in that coffin. So many dreams.

So much despair left behind.

His actual death shouldn't have made a difference. He'd been missing for two months before he died. He'd tossed her away like a used Sunday paper three months before that.

Now Kat shivered in the cold, sleeting rain. She gave her head a vicious shake, warding off the tears that threatened for the first time in days. She straightened her shoulders. *You will not cry.* She had no right to attend the family's service, but she represented someone who did.

Her gaze darted over the ring of mourners. They were folding the flag. In just moments she'd know. They'd give the flag to Miriam, the sister who'd raised him. Miriam. Kat's baby's one chance at a sane life. Anguish wrenched her heart. Sorrow for Max, sorrow for this baby she already loved too much to keep. Kat fought her tears so she could see the woman who held her future — her child's very life — in her hands.

The soldier stopped in front of an older woman and Kat frowned. Miriam was forty-three, fifteen years older than Max. This woman looked a decade older than that. Too old? No. She couldn't be too old. Women had babies in their forties all the time. Bereavement might make her look older.

An even older man supported Miriam, his arm strong and sturdy around her shoulders. Five others surrounded them, forming a protective half-circle around the couple. Two nephews, Max'd said. Nephews with wives, or at least girlfriends? *Grown* nephews? The woman turned her head in response to something her husband said and Kat caught her breath, nearly undone by the naked pain on the face that so closely resembled Max's own. The resemblance was nearly as close as that between her own mother and herself.

So, this was Miriam. So much grief. She must have loved her brother very much. But Kat hadn't expected her to be so old. She'd pictured a warm, loving *younger* couple. For just a moment, she sagged back against the tree.

It's never easy, Kat. Max's words, and before that her mother's. Words to live by. Why would she expect this to be any different?

You don't have a choice. Unless you damn your sweet baby before it even draws a breath.

All true. No choices, no options, except to entrust her innocent child into the hands of fate. No. Better to trust Miriam.

More movement at the graveside. Mourners began to greet Miriam and her husband. Time to go. Kat wouldn't intrude today.But soon. There wasn't much time.

Chapter One

Five Years Later…

Max Crayton eased his car over to the side of the road and shut off the engine. His hands were shaking. His heart pounded hard in his chest and loud in his ears. Too loud. Too hard. He focused on the Dairy Queen, on the trees waving gently in the sweet spring breeze. Home. After too many long years, it was over. He was finally free to pick up his life nearly where he'd left it.

You can't have Kat back.

Regret stung, so sharp and strong he winced. He should go—just start the engine, drive to his sister's house and get it over with. That's what he was here to do. But he wasn't ready. Arrival at Miriam's heralded a new start. *The first day of the rest of your life.* His fist connected with the steering wheel.

It just wasn't that damn easy.

Because arrival at Miriam's also firmly closed the door on his past. That's why he was here, sitting above Bluff River Falls, Wyoming, watching life go on in the valley below. He'd survived the long years because the past was waiting for him. The ultimate reason for what he'd done. His life. Intact. Complete with Kat. Finishing the simple drive to Miriam's would end that fantasy forever.

He closed his eyes, fighting the inevitable moment when the door—that door to *her*—would latch so resolutely behind him. "Kat," he whispered. "Ah, baby, I'd do it so differently...."

Would he?

Faster than a single heartbeat.

Could he?

No.

He'd taken the only path he could. Kat was the most valuable thing he'd lost, but not the only thing.

You knew it going in.

"Not when I agreed," he argued.

Yeah, well, that ship sailed.

Frowning now, he restarted his car. Miriam would help. His sister always had a knack for making him feel better. She'd mothered him when his elderly parents died. Miriam's husband, Doug, died during his "absence" and he wondered how his sister was coping. Most importantly, how would she react to her "dead" baby brother?

He wound through streets as familiar as his childhood, pulling to a stop once again, this time in front of her modest, yellow tri-level. For a long minute he sat, staring at the house, surprised by the pink Big Wheel parked defiantly in front of the porch. A neighbor's kid, probably, as Miriam's two boys were grown and gone now. Thirty seconds later, he sidestepped the trike, and stood in front of the door. He lifted his hand to knock, and let it fall back to his side.

What would he say? "Hi, sis. Surprise! I'm not dead after all." Would she understand that he still couldn't discuss his manufactured death? Would she accept him back into her life? Forgive him?

He lifted his hand again, but the door suddenly flew open, revealing an enchanting pixie of three or four. Perfect little teeth flashed as she grinned at him. "Hiya, Max."

He bit back a frown. She knew him? Long, blond braids swung as she turned her head.

"Mommie, Max is home from Heaven."

While You Were Dead -
Available Now

Timewalker Chronicles Book 2: Silver Storm

Made in the USA
San Bernardino, CA
18 April 2014